M. .... you

So MUCH!

JUSTICE
FOR
DALLAS

ENJOY THE "READ!"

Mark Rua

3/12/17

JUSTICE
FOR
DALLAS

A Marko Novak Mystery

MARK RUSIN
and PRISCILLA BARTON

Loop O Press
Chicago, Illinois

JUSTICE FOR DALLAS
Copyright © 2013 by Mark Rusin
Printed in the United States of America

This is a work of fiction. Names, characters, places, and incidents portrayed in this novel are either products of the authors' imagination or are used fictitiously. Any resemblance to actual persons, living or dead, events, or locales is entirely coincidental.

Cover design by Karen Phillips www.PhillipsCovers.com
Cover photo courtesy of Shutterstock
Book design by Debora Lewis www.arenapublishing.org

ISBN-13: 978-1490399706
ISBN-10: 1490399704

For ATF Special Agents Larry Williams and
Tom Lambert, who left this earth far too soon.

We hope for better things, which shall rise from the ashes.

~Fr. Gabriel Richard, motto for the City of Detroit, 1805

JUSTICE
FOR
DALLAS

NORTHERN CALIFORNIA, EARLY OCTOBER, 1986

1

SHAKIN' THE EARTH, that's what the rumble felt like to Butch, all of them throttled up together and riding in a pack, heading for Guerneville, for the annual rally. Butch Crowley and his Vallejo brothers, his Iron Cobras, cruising north for a three-day party.

Fall was the special time, perfect for the open road, when Butch could see and hear everything. Every day should be like this, everything coming at him like a gift. Like the sound of the Harleys' pipes: most days when Butch heard the roar of the pipes, they sounded like thunder. But on a day like today, riding with his Cobras, with the sunshine pouring out of the sky, they hummed with a low echoing buzz, like being inside a great, restless swarm of bees.

On a day like this, the sun and the breeze meant Butch could feel his skin, could almost feel the tattoos that covered his arms, the flames that raced up toward his shoulders. He loved ink, was nearly sleeved out, wished there was more space for the tats he pictured in his mind. When he moved, flexing his muscles so that the pictures came alive, it was like a movie. In summer, cruising in his biker vest with the Cobra Head patch, his skin was a beautiful custom shirt. The vest, with its secret signs, its flash, advertised Butch's status—Vallejo chapter president. So did his place at the front of the pack, with his best buddy, Chucky Verdugo, riding right beside him. This was the real Butch. This was when Butch belonged inside his skin. It made everything else—all the shit of living in the city, his special duty to the Cobras—worth the trouble.

Gradually, the day got warmer, the sun got stronger. As the pack pulled into Guerneville, heads turned to follow the rumbling procession into the campground. Butch reached up, loosened the bandana around his neck, ran his hand down his pointy black goatee, over his special vest. The Sultan of Harley.

They had arrived.

Maybe a hundred bikers, their girlfriends, full-patch Iron Cobras, the Vallejo club's prospects and hangarounds, were there for the long weekend. Already, music blared from loudspeakers, reefer smoke floated by, and the beer was cold and free-flowing—an endless supply. When they fired up the grills, the smell of seared meat would sharpen their appetites.

Fueled by crank, they could party, party, party for three days straight.

When it was over, the rally would be one beautiful blur.

———

NOBODY COULD SAY for sure what the head count was for the weekend. Somewhere between eighty and ninety, maybe—but nobody, not even the Vallejo chapter sergeant-at-arms, had stayed straight enough to keep track.

Now, late afternoon on the final day, they'd gone through

untold numbers of burgers, hot dogs, smokes, cases of Bud, Jack Daniels, and lines of coke and crank. The party was coming to an end, and people were packing up, taking away their hazy memories and leaving behind a trash-strewn field.

Butch and Chucky stood in the middle of the field, waiting for their buddy Johnny LaSalle. Johnny was supposed to make a delivery, but he was hours late. If Butch hadn't been wasted, he would have been ready to kill the guy. Finally, LaSalle pulled in, killed his engine, dropped the kickstand, and nodded to Butch that he had the goods. Now Butch could get on with things. He had decided maybe an hour ago that he was sick of the party, was glad it was over. It was time for the next thing. He announced to the departing assembly that some of the guys were driving up to Fort Bragg, over on the coast. There was some unfinished business in Bragg that they needed to resolve.

Butch had been raging for a couple of months about a one-time Cobra brother, a guy called Billy Derhammer. Billy's offences were numerous. He'd quit the Vallejo chapter in bad standing and had inked over his Iron Cobras tattoo with "out 1986." He'd been chapter treasurer, and there was money missing from the club till. Plus, he had stepped into the drug territory of another Cobra. Billy was a thief, Butch was convinced of it. The guy was disgraced, out of the club forever, and there was a rule about that: nobody but a full-patch Cobra could wear a Cobras patch or tattoo. Butch couldn't get Billy's disrespect out of his head. It had been whispering to him for weeks; now it was shouting in his ear.

Butch, Chucky Verdugo, Johnny LaSalle, and one other Vallejo Cobra decided to take the green Chevy van. It was an anonymous old junker that had been used to transport food and drink for the rally. They would drive the van north, then west over to the coast. Billy Derhammer had skipped town two months ago, and just yesterday Butch found out where the guy had gone.

It was time to pay Billy a visit.

2

JUST PAST MIDNIGHT the neighbors on Pine Road in Fort Bragg spotted the flames and called 911. The four fire fighters who responded to the emergency call were all volunteers from Fort Bragg. One of them, a twenty-two-year-old just out of the Marines, had signed up only a month ago. He'd been on several practice drills, but this was only his second real call. The other three were local men with families. The oldest, at forty-one, had been designated the unit commander.

With sirens blaring, they figured their response time was pretty good, but in the costly minutes it had taken each of them to report to the station and then get the big truck out to the farmhouse, the structure was fully ablaze, smoke was everywhere, and fire had penetrated the building's interior. Even as the men let out their hoses and began to douse the flames, they realized that much of the building could not be saved. Their only hope was that no one had been home.

Then, as they fought their way inside with the heavy hoses, tramping through blistered, broken glass, falling rubble, a wall of smoke and intense heat, they came across the first body.

It was a little girl, blonde and blue-eyed, not more than five years old. She was lying in a fetal position, clutching a small red Matchbox car in her hand, her pink pajamas soaked in blood. Her throat had been slit ear to ear, almost a decapitation.

The volunteer commander of the four-man unit radioed the dispatcher, telling her to notify the Mendocino County Sheriff's homicide unit. They would have to change tactics, summon their training, fight down their emotions. They would also have to attack the blaze without destroying evidence with hoses, gloves, or boots. Now they were working a murder scene, and almost certainly an arson fire as well.

Then they found the second body. He lay at the foot of the stairs, a teenaged male. The back of his head had been blown away, the entry hole between his eyes. Another bullet had penetrated his chest.

In the kitchen, where the flames had been hottest, was the body of a male, badly burned, a gaping hole in the back of his head.

The woman was also in the kitchen—middle aged, completely naked, burned over most of her body, the left side of her head missing, a bullet hole in the opposite temple.

Four bodies, an entire family.

In this sleepy little northern town, they'd never seen anything like it.

3

BUTCH FELT LIKE he'd spent the past few hours shrouded in a thick black cloud with no way out. This feeling came over him more often than anybody knew, and now it was bad. It was like he'd lost his footing, like he was floating out in darkest space with nothing to grab onto. A long time ago, when he was young, somebody had told him it was insecurity, but these days nobody would dare say such a thing. At least not to his face.

Last night, things had gotten way out of hand. Butch didn't know how it had all gone down so fast. He was even having trouble remembering exactly what'd happened. But it wasn't just him—Chucky was acting crazy, so was Johnny. Maybe something, some outside force, had taken over for them—like they didn't have control, like it wasn't really them doing what they did.

And then there was the blood on his jeans. Jesus Christ, almost like he'd been rolling in it. That was the bad part. And now that he was back in his home, his refuge, Angel was staring at him like he was some kind of crazed animal. Even before she opened her mouth, he said, "Shut up, Bitch." She didn't say a word, not one word. But that was now. What was Angel going to say tomorrow?

He stripped off his jeans, shoved her over to the sink. With her washing, he'd have time to think, make a few phone calls, make sure everybody got it right. Make sure they knew that if he goes down, they go with him. He had something on all of them. Fuck, he had something on everybody he knew. But still, this felt way too public.

That thing he'd heard all his life, "Don't do the crime if you can't do the time," kept running through his head, over and over, like the lyrics to a bad song that he couldn't stop his mind from playing. Like there was a school for criminals, and that one line was the lesson. Repeat this: Don't do the crime, don't do the crime, don't do the crime.... But it wasn't going to go that far. It wasn't going to get outside the club. What were the pigs going to find? Just ashes. Just what the son of a bitch had coming.

4

LAST NIGHT, Marko Novak had made a night of it. Up until last year he'd thought of himself as a party boy, but now he was thirty and respectably employed. Very respectably. He was a Fed, for Christ's sake, a special agent. But yesterday, after a thorny day at the ATF office, his new job and his newly revised opinion of himself didn't stop him. He wanted to drink, and he wanted some fun.

First, there'd been a few beers with the guys at Harrington's Pub, a smoke-filled watering hole across the street from 450 Golden Gate Avenue, the ATF building in San Francisco. Next, there were the after-work cocktails at the Hillside Bar, not far from his house in Novato. Then there was Hailey, a little brunette with a gap-toothed smile. Hailey was a girl he'd seen at the Hillside many times before, always with one guy or another. Last night, though, she'd been alone and was looking around the bar. The minute she appeared on the bar stool next to him, Marko knew he should have said no. Just the way she looked at a guy, the easy way she moved her body, Hailey was the kind of girl who made you think of trouble. A little bit slutty, Marko thought. Not that he had anything against sluts. Compared to what Marko had seen during his time with Las Vegas Metro, Hailey glowed like a comet. And he liked that space between her two front teeth.

They had a few drinks—getting to know each other. The more she drank, the more she talked. At eleven-thirty or so, already past his weekday bedtime, Marko walked Hailey to her little red Mustang, and she followed him home for a nightcap. Did she have to go to work the next day? Marko didn't think so, because after that first nightcap, Hailey had wanted to stay up all night.

Now it was six-thirty, the sky was barely light, and he wished he was still in bed. Preferably without Hailey, who turned out to be a nonstop talker. Instead, he was sitting in the front seat of his partner's car, deeply hung over, drinking lukewarm black coffee from a cardboard cup.

Marko's partner, Larry, had come by for him a half hour ago. Larry was especially alert this morning, making last night's party-boy antics seem all the more stupid. They were driving north on Highway 101, headed to Fort Bragg over on the coast.

Well before dawn, Larry had gotten the ATF call on his pager. There'd been a vicious crime in Mendocino County the night before, and the local homicide detective, a man named Roy Gorky, was overwhelmed and needed some help from the Feds. The crime scene had been torched, and the only evidence left behind were arson and ballistic traces, which were ATF specialties, and this one sounded bad.

Larry reached for the car's lighter, lit a Marlboro, let the smoke drift from his nostrils. They were speeding north along the largely unpopulated highway in Larry's government car, a black 1983 Pontiac Trans Am that had been confiscated from a drug dealer. It was comfortable enough to sleep in, Marko thought wistfully, and it purred. He sighed, deciding he might as well face the day ahead.

"You look a little peaked," Larry said in his raspy voice.

"Peaked?"

"You know, *done in... worn out.*"

"Ah."

"We're not even halfway there yet," Larry said.

"I'll perk up when we see the crime scene," Marko said.

Marko couldn't help envying Larry, who was rugged-looking and cool, with an air of unavailability that Marko had never been able to cultivate. Women found Larry irresistible. Marko didn't know if it was his partner's handsome face or the unavailability that they loved. Marko was nothing if not available. That must have been what Hailey from last night had seen in him. Larry, on the other hand, was the Marlboro Man, smooth and remote, with fingers stained from tobacco. The opposite of peaked.

"So, what was she like, your little friend from last night?"

Marko shook his head. "Shit, if I talked that much, you'd shove me out of the car while it was speeding."

"What'd she talk about?"

"She talked about how wonderful and good-looking I am and how she couldn't stop talking about me—what do you think she talked about?"

"I thought maybe she talked about your housekeeping abilities, or what a good listener you are..."

"Right... actually, she told me everything but her Social Security number. Maybe that too, but by then I'd decided to get my two hours' sleep before you called."

When they cruised through Ukiah, Marko said, "Hey, hey, hey! Slow down. We just passed a donut shop."

"I'm watching my weight," Larry said.

"Yeah, well, I'm not. Pull over."

When Larry first gave him a rundown of what Gorky said they would find in Fort Bragg, Marko groaned inwardly. Now, he was getting more anxious the closer they got to the scene, his first major homicide since joining the ATF. Before he became a Fed, Marko had been a street cop in Las Vegas for four years and had seen a lot, but this sounded worse than anything he'd caught at Vegas Metro.

"They bring in the canines?" Marko asked.

"The dogs hit on accelerants."

"What type?"

"They think maybe kerosene. We'll know this afternoon."

"Bad piece of work," Marko said.

"You got that right, partner."

Larry turned off 101 twenty miles north of Ukiah, at the little town of Willits. From there, Highway 20 headed toward the coast through misty redwood forest, the ancient giants looming overhead. So tall they blocked out the sky.

This was only the third trip Marko had made to Mendocino, but Larry had worked the county many times before. It was thirty-five-hundred square miles of beautiful, coastal California, with very little law enforcement and a perfect climate for the cultivation of marijuana.

"Believe it or forget it, land around here used to be cheap," Larry said.

"When was that?" Marko said. "And why wasn't I in on it?"

"Because you weren't a hippie."

"I didn't have the right outfit," Marko said.

"In the sixties, early seventies, hippies moved up here from the city, started growing the strongest pot in the West. Then they figured out how to make it big business."

"The Emerald Triangle," Marko said.

The Fort Bragg harbor came into view just as the sun was burning off a blanket of silvery fog. The place had been a fishing village and a lumber boomtown long before pot became the cornerstone of Mendocino County prosperity. Now Fort Bragg was a charming little town on the coast with street names like Cedar, Oak, Chestnut, and Fir.

"Drive inland for two miles on Pine Road," Detective Gorky had told Larry. "You'll come to a rural area with a few houses—chickens, goats, all that shit. That's where you'll find the farmhouse. It's a nasty torch job, no question, but nothing compared to what they found inside."

5

SHORTLY BEFORE 9:00 a.m., Marko and Larry located the farmhouse beneath a canopy of redwood trees. The fire was completely dead by then, not even a puff of smoke rising from the charred building. They knew that evidence technicians and the medical examiner had already worked the scene, that the bodies had long since been removed.

The two agents put on boots and gloves before they searched the structure, looking for whatever ballistic and arson material might be left in the building. For the next three hours, they investigated every room, every square foot of yard, the still-intact garage. When there was nothing more to see, they got back in the Trans Am, retraced their route back onto Highway 20, then over to 101. The Mendocino County seat was in Ukiah, forty miles south and east of Fort Bragg. In town, they picked up some sandwiches at a local Mom & Pop, then headed for the county building on Low Gap Road.

They found Detective Gorky in his office at the rear of the building. The grim atmosphere infecting his department since the events of last night was as enveloping as the morning fog in

Fort Bragg harbor; Marko felt it the moment he stepped inside. It was almost enough to make him forget he was hungry.

Gorky was expecting them, with copies of everything he'd received so far. Larry went to speak with the cops who'd spent a hectic, difficult night working the scene. Marko found an empty desk, started sifting through each piece of forensic evidence and the preliminary findings from the medical examiner.

On his third cup of coffee, his ham-and-cheese sandwich a distant memory, Marko sat hunched over a desk piled with papers, a stack of crime-scene photos in his hand. The medical examiner's preliminary report confirmed by blood type that the middle-aged female had been the mother of the two children. Part of the adult male's left bicep had been cut away, and both his arms were broken. His body had been doused with kerosene and lit on fire.

Marko pondered the chest wound to the boy, a through-and-through wound to the upper-left breast. From the crime-scene photos, it looked like the bullet had come from a distance below. He worked trajectory patterns based on the boy's height, figuring that the teenager was shot from below as he came down the third stair from the top. Wounded, the boy fell to the bottom of the stairs, where he was finished off execution-style.

Four projectiles had been used in the attack—two to the boy, one to the man, one to woman—but so far the investigators had found only three, and those were mangled and fragmented beyond recognition. Later, when Marko and Larry finished here, they'd return to the Fort Bragg scene. Marko would make it a point to scour the area at the top of the stairs, looking for the initial bullet that had gone through the boy's chest. Maybe he'd get lucky with that one. But who could slit the throat of a little girl? What did this carnage mean? And in the middle of nowhere?

The lab report confirmed that the accelerant had been kerosene, poured on the body of the male in the kitchen and on the kitchen floor. The assailants wanted the fire to burn quickly.

Gorky's team found a newer-model Harley-Davidson motorcycle in the undamaged detached garage. The California license plate was registered to a William Derhammer.

Four bullet wounds, kerosene, a Harley in the garage. So far, not much to go on. It was a brutal business, ugly even to think about.

When Larry and Roy Gorky weren't looking, Marko slipped a crime-scene photo of the slain little girl into his pocket. It was the saddest thing he'd ever seen, fraught with emotion, but it would help him find who did this. He'd show it to potential witnesses when he needed them to talk. He'd force himself to look at it when he was tired of working the case, knowing it would goad him to seek justice for the child and her family. When it was all over, he hoped he would nail it to the killer's grave.

6

THE DAY HAD been endless. One of those dreary, sordid days that left Marko feeling rootless. Finally, after hours in Fort Bragg, then Ukiah, then Fort Bragg again, he was back in Novato, in the little suburban house he was calling home. He wanted to phone his mother in Chicago, to make sure he indeed had a mother, a human female who had given birth to him thirty years ago, that he wasn't some space alien set down in this place called California for the sake of witnessing the more horrific acts that human beings could perpetrate.

For dinner he'd eaten two pieces of leftover pizza from the fridge. His third beer of the night was resting on the coffee table next to his feet. He was on the couch in front of the television, not seeing or caring what was on.

When Marko was a kid he cared a lot about what was on TV. He'd watch all the cop shows—*Dragnet, Adam-12, Hawaii 5-0, The Untouchables*. He couldn't get enough of them. Law enforcement, he knew, would be cool and never boring—an engaging dream after days spent more or less productively at Our Lady of the Snows grammar school, then Quigley South

High. Besides, he could serve his country, like his dad did driving a tank in World War II. His dad, who told Marko at a very early age that, no matter what, it was all bullshit.

In college Marko majored in law enforcement and, yes, ice hockey, so that he could get where he was today. Today?—the dream of a federal badge come true, after just four years of working the Vegas Strip as a Metro cop, where he'd gotten a Ph.D of street.

He thought about everything that had happened today, which stirred up the rootless feeling again. To lighten his mood, he made himself think about Las Vegas, a place he loved. Just two little words, but they meant so much: sex, gambling, extortion, drugs, pimps, whores, loan sharks, suicide, bail bondsmen, scams, thieves, mobsters, corruption, murder, booze... and no-last-call. But more than all this, Vegas meant blackjack.

Marko had first gone to Las Vegas in 1978 on a three-day gambling junket with his buddy Mike, a fireman from Chicago. Being with the police department or the fire department were the best jobs in the city, but especially being a fireman. Those guys worked twenty-four hours on, forty-eight off, and every fifth shift they would get the day off. It was particularly great if they could get a slow firehouse in a good neighborhood, because then they could rest up for their second job. Most of the guys had other businesses or moonlighted as carpenters and electricians or owned hot-dog stands, so they were making a killing. What a country! Of course, those were patronage jobs in the days of old man Daley. In those days, Marko was hanging around Chicago as a bartender and bouncer at a mobbed-up South Side night club called Pepe's Show Lounge. It was quite a place. Good bands, beautiful women, and Marko was young and single.

In Vegas that weekend with Mike, he hit it off with a pretty little Italian blackjack dealer from the Riviera Hotel. Her name was Louise and she lived in a beautiful townhouse with her little dog Keno, just off the fabulous Strip. The night he met her, they went out for a few drinks when she got off her shift at two in the morning. Louise picked Marko up at Valet in her white T-top Camaro. She was the neatest gal, and the one who told him that the police department there was hiring a lot of coppers.

Marko asked her to mail him the application from that next Sunday's newspaper, and she did. Two weeks after he sent in his résumé, they called him to come out for the test, in September. It was four days of testing—physical agility, written exam, psychological inventory, and oral interview. If you passed all those, you were placed on a list, and pending a full background investigation, you had a good shot at landing a job.

He finished number twenty-six out of eight hundred and fifty applicants, which meant he would get called in the first wave of hiring if the background check went okay. Marko was sure it would, as he'd never gotten caught by the cops doing anything wrong. Not that he didn't break a few rules along the way, but lucky for him he just never got caught.

At the time, he was living in the upstairs apartment in his parents' house on the South Side. That's where he was when the call came in, letting him know he'd gotten the job. He would be sworn in as a Metro police officer on the day after his twenty-fifth birthday, January 16.

His mom and dad thought that he was never going to leave Chicago, but he told them it was the chance of a lifetime. In his heart he wanted to be a Chicago cop, but it wasn't meant to be. Marko wasn't the right color or gender at the time. Besides, Vegas was calling. And Marko knew he could always come back home if things didn't work out. He was so excited he couldn't sleep.

The second week of January, Marko packed up his two polyester suits, put his stereo system and speakers in his 1978 Chrysler Cordoba, and drove with his father to Las Vegas.

They went to the Tropicana Hotel for dinner on his birthday, and later that same night his dad caught a flight back to Chicago. His dad was crying at the airport as they said good-bye. It was only the second time Marko had seen him cry. The other was when Marko was about eight years old and his father got a call that his brother Eddie had died in a car wreck in Stevens Point, Wisconsin.

At the airport, Marko acted like Mr. Tough Guy, but he felt the loss, like he was leaving his childhood behind. The next day he was sworn in as a Metro cop and given a beautiful gold badge with the number 2063 inscribed on the back. That was his badge number and what he, Officer Novak, would be called for the next four years.

It was the beginning.

———

THE PHONE RANG at ten-thirty, just as Marko was starting to unwind.

"Novak," he said into the receiver.

It was Larry, calling to say that Roy Gorky had located the sister of the murdered woman.

"Her name's Trudy Peck. Nice-sounding women, lives in

Santa Rosa. She told Gorky that Billy Derhammer had been an Iron Cobra until a couple of months ago. We're set to talk to her first thing tomorrow."

After he hung up with Larry, Marko took out the crime-scene photo of the little girl, but looking at it was almost unbearable. He started to cry. He couldn't help it.

Outlaw bikers, scum of the earth.

7

WHEN TRUDY PECK answered the door to her neat little Santa Rosa bungalow, she looked like she hadn't slept in a week. She was plump and attractive, on the cusp of middle age, the kind of woman who, most days, would care about her appearance. Her blonde hair was streaked with gold highlights, and her nails were painted pink. But today her highlighted hair hung limply to her shoulders, and her eyes were puffy and red. She wore a light-blue workout suit and bedroom slippers. She told Marko and Larry that she worked for a title company here in town, and that she'd lived in Santa Rosa for the past eight years.

She'd been hit with the worst kind of news. Yesterday, Roy Gorky had taken her to the morgue to identify the bodies of her sister, her brother-in-law, her nephew, and her niece.

"Erin was older than me," she told Marko and Larry. "Two years older."

The three of them were sitting in Trudy's compact living room. Except for the brick fireplace, almost everything in the room was blue. It was all very clean.

"What about the kids?" Larry asked.

"Dallas, Erin's little daughter..." Trudy started to cry. Marko looked over at Larry, who spotted a box of tissues on an end table and handed it to her.

"My nephew Jeremy, he was fourteen," she went on, pulling herself together. "He was a good kid."

"Was Billy Derhammer the father?"

"Dallas's father, not Jeremy's," Trudy said. "Erin and Billy got married six years ago."

"What can you tell us about Billy?" Larry asked.

Trudy sighed so deeply that Marko wondered if she would come back up for air.

"Yesterday, when they wheeled him out, I saw him lying there, what was left of him," she said.

"I know you had to identify them," Larry said.

"I'll never forget it."

"I'm sorry you had to go through that," Larry said.

"It would upset me to say anything against him."

"It's important," Larry said.

There was a photo album on the coffee table. Trudy picked it up. She leafed through it until she came to a wedding picture of Billy and her sister. In the photo, an eight-by-ten that looked like it was shot by a wedding photographer, Billy looked taller than Erin by about six inches, and a hundred pounds heavier. Overweight, Marko thought, but he looked strong. Billy wore a black suit with a Western cut, a nice white shirt, and a bolo tie decorated with a big piece of turquoise. His cowboy boots were polished to a high shine. Erin Derhammer was blonde and pretty. Her flowered dress reached her ankles, and the brim of her straw hat nearly covered her eyes.

"Billy was a good father, until everything went to hell."

"What happened?"

"He started hanging around with a biker gang, the Iron Cobras. You know about them?"

Larry nodded.

"Billy always knew bikers, but not outlaws, not gangbangers. But then, when he got into the Cobras, everything changed. He stopped working, he was never home."

"So who paid the bills?" Marko asked. "Did Erin work?"

"Oh, there was plenty of money. Billy started dealing drugs. Erin didn't have to work."

"You know what he was dealing?"

"It was meth mostly. That's what Erin told me."

She turned a page in the album, to a picture of Trudy and Erin together when they were young. They looked almost like twins.

"Erin wouldn't even talk about it at first. But then finally she just got disgusted and told Billy that if he didn't get out of the biker life, she'd leave and take the kids."

"Did he?"

"Eventually. But it took him a while. Then he started looking around for a real job."

"Was that still in Vallejo?"

"They moved to Fort Bragg and didn't tell anybody where they were going. I thought I was the only one who knew, but I guess the wrong people found out. Billy got a job in construction up there, and Erin said he was serious about changing his life."

"How long ago was this?"

"Two or three months. They wanted to stay in Vallejo, but Erin didn't feel safe there anymore."

"Had something happened?" Marko asked.

"I guess when you're an Iron Cobra, you can't just quit. Some of the Cobras... Erin told me they threatened Billy when he left. The leader, a crazy, violent guy named Butch—Erin was terrified of that guy."

Trudy Peck turned the pages of the album until she came to one filled with photos of her niece. On the top-right side was a picture of Dallas Derhammer blowing out candles on a birthday cake. When Trudy touched the photograph, Marko's hand went to the pocket where he'd put the crime-scene photo of the child.

"Can I see that picture?" Marko asked.

She handed him the album.

He stared at the photo of the little blonde girl in its plastic sleeve. "Cute kid," Marko said, wishing he knew how to be more consoling. He remembered one of his own early birthday parties. His mom had ordered a special cake from the neighborhood grocery store, decorated to look like a hockey rink. The first thing Marko had eaten was the sugar puck.

"Can you believe such a thing? Dallas was only five years old," Trudy said. "I know it was the Iron Cobras that did this."

She took the album from him, reached behind the birthday-cake photo, and pulled out another print just like it.

"Take this," she said, handing the picture to Marko. "I want you to find out who killed my family."

8

IN THE LAW-ENFORCEMENT world, Dexter Poole was what was politely referred to as an informant. To Marko he was a cop's best friend, someone you could turn to in times of need—a snitch. Vegas Metro had practically run on informants, so Marko was well-schooled in the world of snitches.

Dexter was also, Marko remembered, a biker. Probably not an outlaw biker, like Billy Derhammer had been. Just a guy who loved bikes, wanted to talk about them more than most people had time for, who loved everything about biker life on the open road—his chopper, the gear, tinkering with his bike, the runs and rallies, the freedom on two wheels.

A year ago, Larry had arrested Dexter in a Mendocino County marijuana field, and at the time Dexter had been holding a gun. The bust was a big deal for Dexter, Marko knew, because the guy thought of himself as pretty decent, being a Vietnam vet and all. Not long afterward, Dexter moved from the pot-growing fields of Mendocino to the distribution fields of the Bay Area. That was when he agreed to be an informant. It wasn't because he had decided to be on the side of law and order. He just knew that Marko and Larry could get the Feds to pay for information.

Like he told Marko, "Why not? I'm not getting rich selling guns to lunatics or meth to kids, like some of the Cobras I know.

"I'm not your outlaw-biker type," he said. "There's no way I'd make it in the Mongols or the Vagos, or especially not the Cobras."

"Why's that?" Marko asked.

"Those guys, once they get in the club, they give it their absolute loyalty. Cobras, right or wrong. You know what I'm saying?"

Marko nodded.

"Total retaliation for any kind of disrespect. Defending the club, the integrity of the patch, protecting the colors—do or die and all that shit. And sometimes it's die. I heard about guys being shot off their bike because they're wearing some patch they're not supposed to be wearing. It's like the mob, an honor thing. Nobody insults the Iron Cobras.

"The guys who're devoted to the club, the full-patch Cobras, they're mostly assholes. Sure, I know a lot of them and sometimes I hang around the clubhouse, shootin' the shit about bikes 'cause, let's face it, they know about bikes.

"But basically I'm just a hangaround, and that's fine with me."

When Marko left the meeting with Trudy Peck that morning, he reached Dexter by phone at home, persuading the snitch to meet him in a couple of hours at a noisy diner in Novato, far enough from Vallejo to be anonymous. Big, ugly, mean-looking Dexter had gotten there first, taken over a corner booth. When Marko arrived, Dexter was holding the menu in his huge, intimidating hands, ordering a double cheeseburger with everything, extra bacon, a side of onion rings, and a giant Coke. He looked hungry, and they both knew that Marko would be picking up the tab.

"You know about that rally in Guerneville last weekend?" Marko asked.

"I wasn't there, but, yeah, I heard about it."

"And Fort Bragg?"

"I heard some bad shit went down there."

"It was a slaughter."

Just as Dexter's food arrived, Marko went into detail about what had been done to the Derhammer family. Then he pulled out the crime-scene photo of Dallas Derhammer. "This is how they killed the daughter."

"Aw shit," Dexter said, taking the photo from Marko. "I saw this little girl one time with Billy. If those bastards did this to her... Jesus, now they've crossed the line."

"Who're you talking about?"

"It's gotta be the Vallejo Cobras. Billy was in the chapter, but then some shit went down and I think they forced him out."

Dexter paused to load up the burger with more ketchup. "Butch Crowley, the guy who's the chapter president, hated his guts. He thought Billy was a rat, or he'd stolen some money from the club or something. Anyway, Billy left Vallejo a couple of months ago. I haven't seen him since."

"How do I find Butch?"

"He used to live with his girlfriend, maybe still does."

"Who's the girlfriend?" Marko asked.

"Her name's Angel Cruz. Small and pretty but dirty-looking, like all those biker mamas. She's got long dark hair and a tramp stamp on the small of her back—a little blue phoenix."

"How do you know about the tramp stamp?" Marko asked.

Dexter grunted. "Angel used to waitress at a biker bar in Oakland called the Beehive. She liked to smoke dope, snort cocaine. One night, late, everybody was real high, and Butch decided to fuck Angel on the pool table at the bar. A few of us guys were watching, cheering them on. That's when I saw it."

"Nice."

"I'm making her sound like a bad person, but I don't think she is. Nothing like Butch. She's just fucked up from being with that guy."

"Where does she live?"

"Probably still in Vallejo."

"Anything else you can tell me?"

"Only that you ain't gonna get nobody to snitch about this," Dexter said, wiping his face with a paper napkin, balling it up, and throwing it on his empty plate. "What you're gonna get is a wall of silence. A Cobra squeals on his brothers, he signs his own death warrant. The club comes first, and those guys really mean it. If Crowley thought Billy Derhammer was a rat, then there was going to be trouble. Crowley's bad news, a real violent guy. They're not all like that, but he is. You won't get nobody to snitch on Crowley. They'd all be scared shitless. I mean, seeing what happened to Billy and his family…"

Dexter reached for the photo of the little girl on the table. He picked it up in his huge hand, bent over it, staring at the carnage.

"Jesus Christ."

9

THE NEXT DAY, they were back in Ukiah, in a big room at the Sheriff's Department. The minute Marko walked in, he could feel the emotion in the room. The place was charged with it. Detective Roy Gorky was there; so were the police and fire-department investigators, the medical examiner, and the forensic pathologist, all of them hoping to determine what actually happened the night of October 6. The Derhammer crime-scene material—investigative notes, testimony of interviewees, rap sheets, and everything else—was spread out on a large metal table. Photos and a timeline were arrayed on the wall.

They knew that the temperature that night had been sixty-six degrees, with a light mist falling at midnight. The 911 call had come in at 12:35 on the morning of October 7. There was no evidence of forced entry, which probably meant that the doors to the house were open on that misty fall evening, or that the family knew the assailants and let them in. The consensus among them was that there had to be at least three, and maybe four assailants to overpower Billy Derhammer, and his wife,

Erin, and the two children in the way that they had.

Their best reconstruction was that the two adults were somehow surprised at gunpoint, probably in the kitchen area of the farmhouse. Billy's wrists were bound and tied with duct tape to the back rungs of a wooden chair, and the assailants cut a piece of flesh from his left bicep. Was he forced to watch as they ripped the clothes off his wife and violated her, perhaps with the barrel of a gun?

Their teenaged son, Jeremy, upstairs at the time, perhaps yelled or made some noise, surprising the assailants. They shot him as he was coming down the stairs. He wasn't yet dead when he fell to the bottom, so they fired the gun against his forehead to finish him off.

Erin was next, killed in front of Billy. She died instantly from a gunshot wound to the head, just above the right ear. The autopsy revealed that her vagina had been violated by a sharp-edged item, perhaps the barrel of a firearm with its raised sight.

Then five-year-old Dallas appeared in the doorway, having been hiding in her downstairs bedroom. The knifeman, they speculated, chased her back to her bedroom, where he caught her by her right ankle as she tried to crawl under the bed. He pulled her out, slit her throat, and threw her in the corner to die.

Finally, they shoved the gun into Billy's mouth, chipping out his teeth in a perfect circular pattern—the recoil of a handgun shoved down his throat. They drenched his body with kerosene, poured the rest along the kitchen floor, lit a match, and left.

Was that how it went?

The four bullet wounds were consistent with the type of

injury caused by a large-caliber handgun—two into the body of Jeremy, one to kill Erin, a fourth to kill Billy Derhammer. The three projectiles found by the investigators were fragmented and mangled beyond recognition.

Marko had gotten lucky when he and Larry returned to the Fort Bragg scene. He'd studied the trajectory pattern in Gorky's office and had indeed found the fourth projectile, a pristine .357 bullet responsible for the through-and-through wound to the teenaged son as he came down the steps. It was lodged in a wooden doorframe at the top of the stairs. This was a huge find, one of the few positive events in this otherwise clueless inquiry. Marko knew that if they ever found the gun, it could easily be tied through ballistics to the projectile.

No spent shell casings were found at the scene, suggesting that the gun used by the assailants was a revolver. But most .357 revolvers hold five or six shots, and no additional projectiles were found. Had investigators missed a bullet or two somewhere at the crime scene? Had missed shots flown out a window? Did the killers load the gun with only four bullets? If they had more bullets, why knife the little girl and not shoot her?

The investigators had gone over the scene with microscopic care. There was no gun, no knife, no kerosene can. There was no DNA evidence from the assailants, no shoe prints, fingerprints, or tire tracks—no clues about how they got there or how they left. There were no witnesses. What they had was one bullet, a gruesome crime scene, and a Harley-Davidson motorcycle in the garage.

The newer-model Harley, registered to William Derhammer, had been untouched by the fire. It was customized, tricked out in the manner of outlaw bikers. And now there was the medical examiner's report that the fresh knife wound on Billy's left bicep looked like the assailants had surgically removed a tattoo just prior to his death. This was big news for Marko's partner Larry, who had worked several outlaw-biker investigations and knew that this type of carnage was not beneath them. Both the medical examiner's find and the Harley made biker-related sense to the entire team.

Marko told the team about their interview with the sister-in-law, Trudy Peck. Billy Derhammer was a former member of the Vallejo Iron Cobras. He'd finally quit, moved his family to Fort Bragg to escape the club and the violent ringleader, Butch Crowley.

So far, everything led to the Cobras. It was a message killing, Marko was convinced of it.

10

BY NOW, it must have been at least forty-five minutes that Marko and Larry had been sitting in the Trans Am, just south of Vallejo. They were down the block and across the street from an ordinary little ranch-style house, the last known address of Angel Cruz. The house needed a coat of paint, the low wooden fence was missing a couple of boards, and the only thing growing in the scruffy yard was one bedraggled tree. A blue pickup was backed into the driveway, missing its front license plate, so they couldn't run the registration.

Marko and Larry were using the binoculars to scope out the scene, hoping to see some movement, people coming and going from the house, acquaintances of Angel or Butch who might have been involved or who knew what had happened in Fort Bragg. The minute they got out of the car and went up to the house, their cover would be blown. Word would go out that the heat was on. Phone calls would be made from inside to alert others to stay away.

Marko could think of few things more boring than surveillance. At times like this he wished Larry was more of a talker, kind of like Marko himself, who'd been a talker since he was a kid. If you grew up on the South Side of Chicago, talking was part of the culture on the street. In California, handsome guys like Larry could sit around, their muscles showing under their T-shirts. Girls would stare at a hunk like Larry, chase him, buy him drinks. Marko, on the other hand, needed to hustle. When the guys all went out drinking together, he was the one who talked to women, brought them over to the table. Not that Marko was a bad-looking guy; he'd played semi-pro hockey after college and was in good shape—almost six feet tall, just over two hundred pounds. Strong. But not like Larry.

Marko slipped another Jujube into his mouth, passing the time. If he tucked the whole boxful into his cheek, it would last for hours.

Twenty minutes later, they decided it was time to confront Angel and, hopefully, Butch. When they got out and walked up to the house, they saw a pair of scuffed cowboy boots, toes up, sticking out from under the far side of the truck. Dexter mentioned that Butch was a pretty good self-taught auto mechanic, so they wondered if they'd happened on Mr. Scumbag himself.

Marko leaned down to peer beneath the vehicle, said, "You Butch Crowley?"

The guy grunted, threw something heavy down on the broken asphalt, and swung out on his four-wheel dolly, glaring at them. His dark hair was greasy and so was his pointy black goatee; his smokes were stuffed into the torn pocket of his black T-shirt. Bad guy, bad attitude, even before he opened his mouth. His mouth, when he opened it, showed some big gold fillings in front and a few holes behind.

"Depends who the fuck wants to know," he said.

Marko wanted to kick him in the nuts.

The guy looked wiry, strong, and just like the mug shot of Butch Crowley they'd dug out of the files. He held a wrench in one hand, a rag in the other, and barked out, "Well, who the fuck *are* you guys?"

Larry flashed his ATF badge, which shut him up for the moment.

Marko said, "Special Agent Novak, ATF, and this is my partner. You got any idea why we're here?"

Butch grunted no, started to swing back under the truck.

"Hold on, pal," Marko said. "We're here about the murder of Billy Derhammer and his family."

"Oh, that. Yeah, it's a real shame, ain't it. "

"A biker brother of yours gets himself and his whole family wiped out and that's all you can say? It's a real shame?"

Butch glared at them. "Well, you know, shit happens."

"Where were you the night of October 6?" Larry asked.

"I'll have to check my calendar," Butch said as he slid back under the truck.

Marko leaned down, hoping to incite the guy. "Tell me, is Butch your real name, or is that short for Butcher?"

Larry said, "We'll be talking to ya', Bitch," as he and Marko walked up to the front door.

THE SHORT, dark woman with long, full hair who answered the door matched Dexter's description of Angel. What the snitch hadn't mentioned was the look of terror on her face. Behind her, Marko and Larry could hear voices in the room. Someone saying, "I know it's none of my business but..." in a low, insistent voice. A daytime soap on TV.

"We're here about a crime that took place Monday night in Fort Bragg," Larry said. "Did you know Billy Derhammer or his family?"

"I—I never heard of them."

"Did you know that all four of them were murdered on Monday?" Marko asked, and saw Angel's eyes widen. She opened her mouth to speak, shut it. Looked over at the truck.

"The whole family, murdered on Monday," Marko repeated.

"No," Angel said. "I hadn't heard that."

"Were you at the biker rally in Guerneville this past weekend?" Larry asked.

"I was here—right here the whole weekend."

"Do you live here with Butch Crowley?"

"Yeah, Butch lives here."

"Has he said anything to you about the Derhammers?"

"I don't know anything," Angel said in a loud voice, which she seemed to be directing toward the truck. She started to close the door. "Look," she whispered, "I can't tell you anything. I really can't."

Marko looked over at the truck, put himself between Angel and Butch's line of sight, handed her his card. She looked at the truck, slipped the card into her back pocket, and closed the door.

When they got back to the car, Marko said, "That girl's been terrorized."

"You got that right," Larry said.

"What is she, twenty-three, twenty-four?"

"I'd say closer to twenty-seven or twenty-eight," Larry said.

"That punk under the truck was at least one of them," Marko said. "I'd swear to it."

"Well, don't. Don't assume what you don't know," Larry said.

On the drive back to the ATF office, they talked about a plan to track down anybody who'd been at the Guerneville rally—bikers, their girlfriends, hangarounds, anyone associated with anybody there. How many people were aligned with the Vallejo Iron Cobras? How many people had been around that weekend?

More important, how many witnesses were lined up?

Exactly zero.

Dexter had warned Marko about the biker wall of silence, everybody too blindly loyal or, much more likely, too scared to come forward.

So far, Marko realized, Butch's personal reign of terror was having its effect.

11

NIGHTMARES AGAIN. Less than a year with the ATF, and Marko was feeling like there was too much on his plate. The Derhammer homicides were starting to get to him. The past three nights he'd had horrible dreams about them, tossing in his sleep, waking up in a cold sweat.

One of the reasons Marko had wanted a federal badge was so there would be time to investigate and plan his moves, and almost never have to go alone on anything. When he was a cop with Vegas Metro it had been a different story. Then he'd been a street cop, and for a street cop, when the bell rings you go, often alone, no stopping to reflect, doing whatever it takes, that moment, to enforce the law. One call, you might be consoling a lost child at a shopping mall. The next, you're speeding to a hot gun call, hoping not to get killed while putting your life on the line for a complete stranger. Street cops. They were all heroes in Marko's book.

Now Marko had the time to plan, but it didn't seem to be getting him anywhere. Prosecution? They wouldn't get to first base without some hard evidence. And if they didn't get something soon? Well, that was the fear. Witnesses forget, after all—cases grow cold, other ATF cases need to be worked.

Tonight, exhausted, Marko turned on the TV. The movie channel was showing *The Sting*, one of his all-time favorites. The film was maybe a dozen years old and he'd already seen it three times. Newman and Redford, a couple of grifters, going for the long con and winning.

Was it okay, Marko wondered, for a copper to root for criminals who played on other people's greed?

Only if nobody got hurt.

He loved Johnny Hooker's line when he was getting together with the hit girl: "You know me. I'm the same as you. It's two in the morning and I don't know nobody."

Marko Novak, movie critic. He liked the sound of it.

When Henry said to Hooker, "You not gonna stick around for your share?" and Hooker said, "Nah. I'd only blow it," Marko knew it was time to turn off the set and head for bed.

Instead, he fell asleep on the couch, as dead to the world as Hooker's friend Luther, Scott Joplin's piano rags keeping time in his sleeping brain.

12

ANGEL HAD BEEN sitting around the Vallejo house for days, doing nothing, feeling desperate and bored. Late in the afternoon Butch went out to meet his buddies, telling her not to leave the house. When he was out the door, Angel waited a few minutes to make sure he'd really left; then she tried calling her girlfriend Loretta in Vegas. She had tried Loretta's number maybe ten times, whenever Butch left her alone for a while, but there'd been no answer. She and Loretta had been friends since grade school, but they hadn't spoken in four or five months, and Angel didn't even know if she had the right phone number.

Butch had hit Angel again last night, a nasty blow to the side of the head, and now her right eye was swollen and her jaw was sore. She knew Butch's temper better than anyone, but this was something different. He was acting crazy, like he'd gone totally over the edge.

In the bathroom cabinet, Angel found some Demerol, courtesy of Butch's drug dealings. She took one, then later another one, but now she was in pain again and embarrassed to leave the house. Anyone who saw her would know she'd been beaten up.

It had been almost a week since that night when Butch came back to the house with blood all over his favorite blue jeans. It was an awful night, the worst she could remember. Then, two days later, those cops had come by. One of them had handed her his card: Marko Novak, Special Agent, ATF. She was glad she'd kept the card, even though it was taking a chance. Anything she did or said these past few days, even breathing, was taking a chance.

Angel was pretty sure she knew what had happened that night. Butch made her scrub the jeans, told her he'd kill her if she said anything about it, so she just shut up and played dumb. She'd gotten good at that around him, waiting for the chance to get away.

After maybe ten rings Loretta picked up the phone.

"Loretta, it's Angel." Angel started sobbing when she heard Loretta's voice.

"What's the matter, girl?"

"I gotta get away from here, from Butch, right now."

"Well, you can come here. You got a car?"

"No."

"Take the Greyhound bus. I'll pick you up at the station."

Loretta told Angel that she was living about a mile from the Vegas Strip, gave her the address of the apartment building and the phone number of the bar where she worked, said to call as soon as she got to town.

Angel didn't stop to think about it, not even for a minute. As soon as she hung up the phone, she ran through the house, getting some of her stuff together. She'd have to leave almost everything, but at this point it didn't matter. She grabbed a bag, jammed whatever clothes and personal stuff she could into it. Yesterday, she had found over two thousand dollars in a drawer under some of Butch's T-shirts. She took four hundred. Butch had told her that Billy Derhammer was a thief; that's why he'd gone after the guy. As Angel slipped the money into her bag, she knew she had to stop thinking about all the blood, about what Butch did.

Tucking her hair under a baseball cap, wearing a pair of sunglasses to cover her swollen eyes, she opened the door, looked up and down the street, and ran.

13

TONIGHT WAS GAME Three of the World Series at Fenway Park, Mets versus the Red Sox. Marko was hoping to catch some of the game later. It was only Tuesday, but he thought he deserved a few hours off. He was pretty sure that Boston would pull it off this year, throwing off the Curse of the Bambino once and for all. They were already ahead by two games, and it was looking good.

He wished it was his own White Sox that were playing. When Marko was a kid, the White Sox held batboy contests—write a letter to the *Chicago Daily News*, telling them "Why I want to be the White Sox batboy." In 1969, when Marko was fourteen, his buddy Al won the writing competition. Al arranged it so that Marko filled in for the Jewish batboys, who couldn't work Saturdays. Marko was a good ballplayer, had been a starter on his high-school varsity team when he was only a freshman. He impressed the Sox clubhouse manager and got a steady job because of his work ethic. Cleaning spikes, washing uniforms, and picking up dirty jockstraps. Marko didn't mind. This was the bigs, and he met a lot of cool people.

Besides, he was making six bucks a game—ten bucks for a doubleheader. Not bad for a fourteen-year-old.

One day, early in his batboy career when he was on the field during batting practice, Luis Aparicio screamed at him for turning his back to the batter. Good advice and lesson learned. Luis just didn't want him to take a line shot to the back of his head.

Another time, Marko asked Wilbur Wood to throw him a knuckle ball.

Wilbur said, "Sure, kid. Go put on the mask."

Marko said, "C'mon, just throw it. I can catch it."

Marko was defiant. Besides, he'd borrowed the pancake catcher's mitt from Duane Josephson. The mitt was so big that Marko was sure he couldn't miss. Wood threw the knuckler. It fluttered two feet and Marko tipped it but it split his lower lip wide open. Blood everywhere, so Marko got the towel and applied direct pressure. When the bleeding stopped, he went back out there and asked for another knuckler. Wood obliged and took a little off.

This time Marko caught it.

————————

EARLIER IN THE DAY, Dexter had finally given Marko a call, telling him he'd gotten into the Iron Cobras Vallejo clubhouse.

"Hey, Marko," Dexter said. "They let me back in."

"How'd it go?"

"Well, you know, I'm laying the groundwork. It's like I'm on a mission, given that photo you showed me of the little girl."

"I hear you," Marko said.

"And if you can see your way clear to advancing me

something, I could use some cash," Dexter said.

"I'll see what I can do," Marko said. So much for Dexter's mission, Marko thought. "What happened?"

"When I got there, there were five guys, including me," Dexter said. "A couple of prospects, one guy was a hangaround like me, and one of them was a full-patch guy. Everybody was sitting around, shootin' the shit, but it just seemed like there was an elephant in the room or something. I mean, nobody was saying a single word about the Derhammer thing. And I wasn't gonna mention it.

"Then later Butch blows in and everybody clams up. I mean, suddenly the vibe changes from five guys hanging out, drinking some beer, to major paranoia. Butch starts slamming stuff around, looking for a part for his bike or something. He can't find what he'd looking for, so he yells at the prospects, telling them that if they wanna get into the club, or if they even wanna get back into the clubhouse, they'd better get the fuck off their asses and find it.

"The prospects know they gotta do shit like that, but one of them, this guy Joey, gives me a look, like he's saying, 'Yeah, Butch is chapter president and all, but he's an asshole and is this really worth it?' I just kinda shrugged at him. The thing is, they're all afraid of the guy.

"Maybe ten minutes later, Butch storms out. The guys tell me that Butch's girlfriend left him, walked out when he wasn't there, took some of his money. Nobody, they say, takes anything that belongs to Butch. Ever. Butch was in a total rage about it, said he couldn't believe she'd show him that kind of disrespect."

Marko thought, *Good for her, I hope she makes it.* Maybe if Angel was no longer under Butch's thumb, she'd be willing to talk. The problem now was that Marko had no idea where to find her.

"Anybody know where she went?" Marko asked.

"Nope. And I guess Butch don't know either."

That was a very good thing, Marko thought. If Butch knew, Angel might be dead by now.

LAS VEGAS

14

ANGEL FELT LIKE she'd been saved, landing at Loretta's. After the long nighttime ride through the desert, where she watched the stars through the bus's big windows, shining like they never did in Vallejo, they'd finally pulled into the Las Vegas Greyhound station on South Main Street.

It was early morning in the seedy downtown area of Vegas—vagrants hanging out in front of the station, a bail-bond office and the Clark County jail across the street—when Angel stepped off the bus. She found a pay phone, called Loretta at home. Her friend pulled up twenty minutes later in an old white Chevy, and they took off for Sierra Vista.

Loretta lived in a crummy apartment building, everyone around here either a pimp or a whore. Still, whatever it took to get away from Butch. Angel almost couldn't believe she'd made it over to Vegas alive. The apartment's kitchen and living room were separated by a big island where they could eat sitting on bar stools. There was a tiny second bedroom where Angel slept. She'd brought almost nothing, but Loretta lent her some clothes and makeup.

During the day, Loretta was mostly at home. At night she had a gig at Teddy's, a bar on Flamingo Road. She told Angel that one of the cocktail waitresses had just quit, so Angel went over there with Loretta to see about working, all cleaned up, with her makeup just right. Teddy gave her a waitressing job right off.

Lucky.

Teddy's was a dimly lit bar but nice. The back room was private, for lap dances and whatever else went on. That's where Loretta worked, making five hundred dollars a night, and that was after Teddy took his fifty-fifty split.

In the front room, Angel made almost two hundred dollars her first night serving drinks. The customers were mostly locals, all different types but no bikers, as far as Angel could tell. It was a change from the Beehive in Oakland, and she liked it that way.

Loretta told Angel that the dancing was easy work. "You just pretend that the guys are cute, that their gut doesn't hang over their belt and their breath doesn't smell."

Loretta laughed when she said it.

Angel thought she could get into dancing, except that her tits were too small. She and Loretta were a lot alike—small and dark, good hair, showing nice white teeth when they smiled. Men liked that. But Loretta had the curves. Angel could save up, she thought, get implants. Did you have to do tricks if you were a dancer? But she was sick of being on the game, which is how she'd come to think of her time with Butch. Maybe stay with waitressing.

Teddy didn't want them to work more than three nights a week, but still, the money was good. Was there any way she could have a straight job and survive? What would she do? She'd been on her own since she was sixteen, hadn't gotten past the tenth grade. Hadn't seen her family in Redwood City since then. Didn't want to, either.

At least for now she was staying off drugs and booze, liked having a clear head. Loretta was mostly clean too, and that helped.

Here in the desert the sun was out every day. Every night, the Strip was lit up with a million lights. She decided she liked it. She liked the dry air and the blue sky. She tried not to hate Butch but wondered what had made her stay with him back in Vallejo.

Here in Vegas she felt like she'd been handed a new life.

15

MARKO KNEW HE needed a break. His sleep wasn't getting any easier, the nightmares weren't letting up, and the Derhammer case seemed to be going nowhere. If he went to Vegas for a weekend breather, things might turn around.

He caught a Friday-evening flight, headed straight for his favorite casino as soon as he got off the plane. A few hours at the blackjack tables and things would start to look right again. It had always worked before—the lights, the sounds, a comfortable place to sit, the chips in their neat stacks, the jingle-jangle of the slots for background music, nothing to think about but the cards. His own little green-felt paradise. A new beginning each time he sat down to play. And it was Vegas, the town he loved. Nothing better.

He took a stroll around the smoky, noisy casino, looking for a table that seemed right. Past the baccarat, just after the roulette, there was one with possibilities, and he stopped to watch the action. A friendly dealer, no drunks, no goofs, no slowpokes. An empty seat at third base, his favorite place to sit.

He felt in his pocket for the session money he'd brought—

four hundred bucks. He sat down, bought in, got his chips, heard their soft click.

Right off, Marko caught a short streak, then a few minutes later another one. Staying on the upside for now, at least until the odds caught up with him.

The thing about blackjack, Marko realized, it always made him feel like a high-roller. It was action, just like being a cop, and he was in the middle of it. He didn't have the chops to be a card-counter, not with random shuffles and four decks in the shoe, but he knew when to hit, when to stand, when to split and double down, when to surrender. Every time he finished in the money, sticking to basic strategy, beating the house, it was a thrill. But losing—well, in a Vegas casino, losing was a given. He just didn't want to be stupid about it. He had standards, like for law enforcement. Like being sober when he played. Not playing sober? May as well just stuff your stake in an envelope and mail it to the casino.

Yeah, he was on the upside for now, but then Marko misplayed his hand. He lost focus when the woman he'd met three weeks ago—her name was Marnie—came into his mind. With blackjack, either he should be totally there with the cards, feeling that edge, or he should pack it in. Surrender and walk away. But it was hard not to think about her.

The woman, Marnie Keith, had been sitting in the bar near Gate 8 at the Oakland Airport. The minute he spotted her across the room, he knew she was special. He'd never seen anyone like her. She was sitting alone, her legs crossed, a glass of white wine in front of her. Marko had stopped at the bar for a beer, the last time he'd flown to Vegas for a lost weekend.

She was gorgeous in a low-key way, and sexy. So good-looking that Marko was intimidated. Sophisticated, that was the word for it—high heels, silk blouse, a suit that fit her like a second skin. But friendly, easy to talk to. Sometimes it was hard to get a woman like that into a conversation. With her it felt... *what?* Cozy?

She told him she was an account coordinator with a big cosmetics company, that she worked in San Francisco, Monterey, and Carmel. Marko thought this explained why she looked the way she did, everything about her beautiful and perfect. Her fair skin, her hands, her red fingernails, her dark hair.

He put on the big-time charm, having fun talking in the bar. He told her things about himself and his job that he never told strangers. For Marko and the guys he worked with, for all the ATF Special Agents for that matter, one of the job requirements was to keep things close to the vest. It was why the agency was always moving them around, and part of how they were effective. They stayed away from the neighbors, they didn't tell people what they did, and they certainly didn't hand out their business cards to beautiful women in bars, unless of course they couldn't help it.

"So you're a special agent," she said, reading the ATF card that Marko handed her.

Marko thought she said it like she was impressed, but maybe that was just her way. He stopped himself from bragging about his work, said, "My dream job."

She smiled at him. Her teeth were perfect. Her lips were perfect.

"You catching the Vegas flight?" Marko asked, thinking it would be nice to be in the same town with Marnie Keith.

"I'm waiting for an arrival," she said.

"I'm headed over to Vegas for a few days, ATF business," Marko said, keeping his blackjack jones to himself. "Can I call you when I get back, maybe have another drink together?"

"I'd like that."

Half an hour in a bar, one drink. That's all it had been, but he felt like it had changed everything.

Then, the very next week, the Fort Bragg thing happened and he couldn't bring himself to pick up the phone and call. He was afraid that if they got together he might talk about it. Wouldn't that be great first-date material. *If* she really did want to see him again. She'd given him her business card, though. Not just her phone number on a cocktail napkin, which could be any number. No, he thought she wanted him to call.

———————

AT CAESAR'S PALACE, a beer in front of him, Marko sat in the casino's huge sports book watching Game 6 of the World Series on one of the big-screen TVs. As they headed to the bottom of the tenth, Marko was thinking for sure that the Red Sox were going to become World Champs. With two outs it felt like the party was about to start in Beantown. Then Carter singled to left. Mitchell singled to center. Ray Knight was down in the count 0-2 when he singled to center, moving the tying run to third base.

Marko suddenly thought, *Holy shit... is this happening?*

Next, a wild pitch and the game was tied. Then Mookie Wilson's ball slowly rolled up the first-base line and through Billy Buck's legs. Ray Knight scampered home and jumped on home plate with both feet! Can you believe it?

Suddenly, out of nowhere, it was Mets win! Mets win! Mets

win! The shouting and screaming in the sports book was deafening.

Jack Buck was roaring: "The ball went right through the legs of Buckner, and the Mets with two men out and nobody on have scored three times to bring about a seventh game, which will be played here tomorrow night. Folks, it was unbelievable. An error, right through the legs of Buckner... three in the tenth for the Mets. They've won the game 6–5 and we shall play here tomorrow night! Well, open up the history book, folks, we've got an entry for you."

Wow.

When the noise finally settled down, all Marko could say was "the poor bastard." Nobody would remember that the Red Sox left fourteen men on base that night. And Buckner would be a goat for the rest of his life, especially if they lost Game 7.

The thrill of victory, the agony of defeat. Amazing.

16

ANGEL HAD STARTED working Wednesday, Friday, and Sunday nights at the bar. She asked Teddy for more work, but even three nights was a stretch for him. He said he wanted variety for the customers.

During the day, mostly she would be in the apartment, watching soaps or maybe sitting outside by the crummy pool. She liked to take a cup of coffee out there, sit in the sun for half an hour, dip her feet in the water. Salsa, the next-door neighbor, a working girl with a head of long blonde curls, would sometimes come outside and sit with her. Reggie, a skinny drag queen with a heart-shaped face who performed at a club called La Ronde, would gossip with Angel about Vegas show biz.

Sometimes Angel walked over to the Strip, which was maybe a mile from the Sierra Vista apartment, just looking around, taking in the bright lights, the action, the street life. Then she'd walk through a casino, drop some money in a slot. But sometimes being out in Vegas was too much like working, and she wanted to think about something else.

Teddy's wasn't a bad place to work, though. She even

looked forward to going there. It was one of the cop joints in Vegas, with a lot of guys from Metro hanging out at the bar. They were fun, and they left good tips. Teddy controlled the action in the back room; the Metro guys all knew what was going on but didn't mind. They all drank for free. Vegas was its own kind of place with its own rules, and the guys from Metro knew that better than anyone.

The nights she worked at Teddy's, guys always asked Angel for dates. It happened several times a night. Cute guys, funny guys, rich guys, cops—whoever they were it didn't matter. Right now what she wanted was to be on her own.

Teddy spent most of his time at the bar, but he lived in a big flashy place out in Henderson, ten miles south of the Strip. It was remote with lots of land around it, and he called it his compound. He let a couple of the dancers from the bar live there for free, loved having good-looking, long-legged women hanging on each arm. He thought of himself as kind of a Vegas Hugh Hefner, even though he was short and dumpy and his hairpiece sometimes moved when he talked.

Angel and Loretta went out to the Henderson compound for a pool party one afternoon. The place was decorated more like a showy, low-rent Florida resort than a house, with white shag carpeting, walls the color of fruit—lime green, orange, pomegranate—and a big tank of tropical fish in the living room. There was a waterfall flowing into the swimming pool, and a big hot tub that was elevated so you could see the bright lights of the Strip in the distance. Drinks were served by girls wearing bikinis, like bunnies, like it was still the seventies.

"You girls want somethin' to drink?" one of them asked Loretta and Angel when they sat down near the shallow end.

The bunny woman was about six feet tall, with big hair all frosted and curled, falling down her bare back. One of Teddy's girls.

Teddy was all about tits and ass, but not a bad person. Angel had known a lot worse, felt lucky to have landed at Teddy's Bar.

If he'd just let her work Saturday nights.

17

"YOU'RE MARKO NOVAK, aren't you," Angel said, coming up to where Marko was sitting at the end of the bar, a tray of drinks in her hand.

"That's me. You're..."

"You don't remember me, do you?" Angel said, setting the tray down on the bar next to him.

"Sure, I do," Marko said, searching for a name.

"I even know your phone number," Angel said. "It's 557-2800."

"That's the ATF number. Wait a minute..."

When she finally told him who she was, Marko couldn't believe that Angel Cruz had just walked up to him at Teddy's Bar. He knew from Dexter that Butch's girlfriend had left Vallejo, but Marko had no idea she'd made it over to Vegas.

When he had questioned Angel that day at her Vallejo house, all he saw in her was terror. In the bar tonight she looked all dolled up, like a different person. Of course, the lights were pretty dim in Teddy's. That was an excuse he could give himself for not recognizing Angel Cruz, the woman who might be a central witness in the biggest case he'd ever worked.

"You working here?" Marko asked.

"Three nights a week."

"You doing okay?"

"Pretty good," Angel said.

"Can you give me a few minutes so we can talk?" Marko asked.

"Not now," Angel said.

"When?"

"Not tonight."

"What about tomorrow?"

"I'll be back working here on Sunday. Sunday would be okay. Five-thirty, before I start work," Angel said, picking up the tray.

"I'll be here."

———————

TEDDY'S BAR WAS set back off Flamingo Road, not known to tourists, a place for the locals to hook up, and Marko had always loved it. It was where the casino babes, the dealers, and the showgirls came after work. When Marko had been a Vegas cop in uniform, it was a heaven of free drinks and gorgeous women. It was where he did his best work.

Marko figured it was all about the uniform. All the women he met back then loved it. Casino cocktail waitresses, all of them tall and long-legged, made to wear skimpy outfits, girls who played the players like nobody's business. The more drinks they ran, the more money they made—along with the house, of course. And the dancers, stars in their own dream world, getting some time on stage in front of the bright lights so they could feel beautiful. The Metro uniform made them feel safe and secure in phony little Sin City. If they only knew.

Marko Novak, confirmed bachelor. He still kept a little black book of phone numbers. He knew it was partly the temptation of his visits to Vegas, partly the ATF atmosphere where normal kinds of attachments didn't count, but that's all he thought he wanted—one beautiful woman after the next, a cop job that was all action, a life in the moment. Not having to worry about anybody but himself.

Yeah, that's what he wanted, all right. At least until three weeks ago when he met Marnie Keith. He hadn't even called her yet, and here he was fantasizing about her again. It was like he'd been taken over by a force of nature. God, it felt like forever since he'd seen her in that airport bar in Oakland.

Marko sighed.

Commitment, it was such a dirty little word.

He took out his little black book, so lovingly accumulated, and leafed through the pages. What would it be like to throw it away?

18

SUNDAY MORNING, Marko attended the church of blackjack, finishing in the money but just barely. Later on, around lunchtime, when he was taking a break from the action, he ran into some Metro guys at the Tower of Pizza. It was a favorite old haunt, where his buddies had thrown his going-away party when he left Vegas for the Bay Area to become a Fed.

From the pizza tower, the guys all moved on to the Sahara Saloon at the corner of Boulder Highway and Sahara Avenue, where Jigs the bartender let Metro cops drink beer all day for a five-dollar bill, which he would pocket. Jigs loved Vegas cops, knowing he wouldn't get robbed with Metro there.

The guys were shooting the breeze, drinking beer, talking shit. Marko started telling them about a hot summer night maybe five years back when he was still with Metro and had pulled graveyard shift.

He'd logged onto his unit as he did every shift, "1 John 12," checked his vehicle, and rolled out of the South Substation at around 10:30 p.m. There were some calls backed up, as usual, but for a Thursday night it wasn't too bad. His first was a domestic disturbance, and his backup, 1 John 3, was rolling his way. When Marko pulled up to the building, even from the street he could hear a female screaming. He knew he was supposed to wait for backup, but 1 John 3 was only a few blocks away. As he approached the apartment's screen door, he saw a man beating a screaming female, straddling her on the living-room couch.

Marko entered the room, yelled, "POLICE! Stop!"

The guy turned around, muttered, "Fuck you, asshole!" and continued to beat away at the woman as though Marko wasn't there.

Marko took a step back, calmly asked 1 John 3 for his E.T.A., and heard, "1 John 3 arrived."

The woman's face was bloody and beat to shit, and as 1 John 3 entered the front door the two of them knew they had no choice. Marko's thoughts were to get this guy stopped and handcuffed without him snatching Marko's gun.

Gun retention, Marko reminded himself.

Then Marko hit the guy high, 1 John 3 hit him low, and the fight was on. They had to get him cuffed, and as the two of them tried rolling the guy over, Marko saw the woman get off the couch.

"Hey, get back here!" Marko screamed when she disappeared around the corner, muttering to herself.

Now Marko had one eye on the asshole, trying to help 1 John 3 cuff him, and one eye on the corner where the woman went. This was a small, funky, second-floor apartment with a sliding glass door to a balcony. They almost had the cuffs on EGOR when this crazed, bloody woman came running around the corner with a butcher knife raised above her head.

Marko screamed, "MIKE! [aka 1 John 3]." Then he just snapped. He didn't know where he got the strength, but he tackled the goofy bitch and ran her ass out through the sliding glass door. The balcony railing probably saved her life. Glass everywhere, and all he could think of was what a nut he'd been for trying to help her out. Marko knew this cop stuff was a thankless job, but come on!

Needless to say, Mr. and Mrs. Asshole both went to jail and, as luck would have it, they were married and of course she refused to press charges. Marko booked her on Assault with a Deadly Weapon on a Police Officer, and that was that.

———————

THE METRO GUYS were on their third or fourth beers when Marko looked at his watch, remembering that he had to get to Teddy's. He had made an appointment with Angel when he'd seen her there on Friday. She told him if he came in before her shift, they could talk for a few minutes.

When he got to Teddy's twenty minutes later, she was sitting at a table in the back, drinking a soda. Marko felt like he needed coffee but then remembered what the coffee was like at Teddy's and instead ordered a Coke. They waited for his soda to arrive. Marko noticed that Angel wore big gold hoops in her ears, almost too big for such a small person, but he thought they looked good anyway. Around her neck was a gold chain with a cheap-looking pendant that spelled out her name.

Angel told him how she'd gotten over to Vegas—running out on Butch, the all-night bus ride over here, staying with her friend Loretta but not giving Marko the address. Looking over her shoulder. Well, that was smart, he conceded. Marko was beginning to revise his opinion of Angel, to think her as smart in a lot of ways—except for getting together with Butch Crowley.

"You heard anything from Butch since leaving Vallejo?" Marko asked.

"Some bikers came in here the other night," Angel said. "Teddy wasn't too happy about it. He doesn't like them and the customers don't like them. I didn't tell him about Butch," Angel said.

"You think they were connected to Butch?" Marko asked.

"It feels like every biker is connected to Butch."

"But do you think they were in here because of you?"

"They were looking me over, whatever that means. It makes me feel like I should leave town or something."

"Running away," Marko said.

"I just got here. I just finished running away."

"I know," Marko said. "We'd all be better off with Butch out of the picture."

"What do you think I can do about it?"

"We don't have a single witness for the Derhammer murders."

"That's because everybody's afraid to say anything."

"I know that. But I also think you know something that could help us get to him."

"I'm not going to get killed for it."

"We'll protect you."

"Protect me? In your dreams, maybe," Angel said.

"We could get you into witness protection."

"If you think you can protect me then you don't know the Cobras. They're like dogs after a bone. They don't give up. Ever."

"Whoever killed this family," Marko said, "tortured Erin Derhammer and raped her with the barrel of a gun. They shot and killed the teenage son. They shoved the gun into Billy Derhammer's mouth and pulled the trigger. They killed the little girl—a five-year-old—by slitting her throat." Marko saw Angel flinch when he mentioned the knifing and ran his hand over his throat. "Then they set fire to the house to cover it up. And we don't have a single witness."

Angel looked at him for a long moment.

"You gotta do the right thing here, Angel. Do you really think this scumbag should be left alone to walk the streets?"

She finished her soda, got up, told him she had to get to work.

———

AFTER ANGEL LEFT the table, Teddy came over and sat down with Marko.

"What's up?" Teddy asked.

"Just talking to Angel about some shit in her neighborhood. She's a good kid."

"Doing fine here so far," Teddy said.

"You ever get any bikers in here?" Marko asked.

"The other night. These assholes, never seen 'em before. You know my bar, Marko, we don't cater to that type. I mean, most of the time, every third guy in here's a cop. What would scum like that want with this place?"

That's what Marko wanted to know.

19

FABIAN MARGULIES SAT at his big polished-mahogany desk and brushed an imaginary piece of lint off his midnight-blue silk pajamas. His accountant had just left, and Fabian was more than happy to put away any thoughts of business. He was, after all, an epicure, someone for whom the bottom line was not a particularly compelling topic of conversation. Now he was thinking about opening a good bottle of pinot noir and contemplating what the cook was fixing for dinner. He was also thinking about his law-enforcement friend Marko Novak, who would be arriving in a few minutes to join him.

Fabian liked Marko. A sensitive tough guy, interesting but—what? Maybe *unformed* was the word. Or maybe the unformed part was what made him interesting. So many contradictions to Marko. The bar girls, the blackjack habit, his no-last-call drinking. But also his ambition. Fabian knew that Marko wanted to climb the ATF ladder, succeed as a Fed, maybe go on to work in D.C. Pull himself up by his bootstraps; that is, if he didn't first fall on his face, drunk in Sin City. Fabian thought Marko could be a character out of the movies. Maybe someday he'd even learn how to dress for the part.

Besides, Marko had a very good appetite, even when he didn't know exactly what he was eating. Fabian liked that in his friends. And there was also the police gossip. Fabian loved it— the undercover stuff, the Las Vegas County Club shootout where Marko was almost killed, the current antics of the mob guys who ran Vegas, Tony "The Ant" Spilotro from Chicago and his Hole in the Wall Gang of burglars, even the hookers who walked the gritty Strip. Marko could tell a copper tale better than anyone.

They'd first met when Marko was still with Metro, and Fabian needed some help with an unwanted guest. Marko had known when to be discreet; when something was a matter for police attention and when it didn't need to be. Just as long as nobody got hurt. Since then, they'd been friendly. And Fabian was able to help out Marko from time to time. After all, he knew everyone in town, and what they were up to. He played ball; so did Marko.

Marko had called earlier in the evening for one of their usual Vegas get-togethers when Marko was visiting. Fabian invited him to come by for a drink before he headed back to the Bay Area. It was a ritual between them. Juana the cook would fix some mildly exotic appetizer—something involving fiddlehead ferns, or maybe eel—and Fabian would open an interesting bottle, daring Marko to ask for his drink of choice; Fabian could barely manage to utter the words *brandy and ginger-ale*. They'd gossip, trade information, chew over old times.

Fabian went over to his vintage ebony Bosendorfer—he thought of the piano as his fat black girlfriend—sat down and played a few bars of "Anything Goes." He'd once heard Marko refer to him as the Lounge Lizard. Way back, there would have been some truth to that description, but life had gotten a whole lot better in the past ten years. Money, Fabian thought, was simply wonderful. He had almost everything he wanted. Almost.

NORTHERN CALIFORNIA

20

WHEN MARKO WALKED into the ATF office late Monday morning after his weekend in Vegas, his partner Larry, his supervisor, and his desktop all greeted him with items needing immediate attention. If he hadn't made the connection with Angel, he might have regretted the time off, but Marko knew that finding Angel was vital.

Plus, there'd been that great meal at Fabian's. Marko didn't know exactly what it was he'd eaten last night, but it was delicious. And there was the two hundred dollars he'd won at blackjack. All in all, a worthwhile trip.

Angel, Marko reflected, hadn't exactly been forthcoming at Teddy's, but at least now he knew where she was. At least now there was some hope for a witness in the Derhammer case. Before he left last night, he had asked Teddy, as well as one of his Metro buddies, to keep an eye on her.

Marko told Larry about the meeting with Angel, and they discussed turning her against Butch.

"Your buddy Dexter called this morning," Larry said.

"My good man Dexter the snitch," Marko said.

"He couldn't wait till you got here, so we chatted about this and that—old arrests, trafficking in marijuana, illegal firearms possession. Surprisingly, he mentioned that he needed money."

"Very surprising... "

"So I said we needed him to wear a wire," Larry said.

"And?"

"He said okay."

"You set it up?"

"Dexter's lined up for tomorrow, and I got consent from the Division. If Butch makes an appearance at the clubhouse, we'll go for it."

Marko made the arrangements for the surveillance vehicle, which was an undercover ATF van equipped with listening and recording equipment. Dexter, they decided, would wear the wire in his boot rather than on his chest. The Iron Cobras were notorious for their paranoia, and a bug in the boot would be less likely to be discovered. Marko and Larry would listen and record from the van a short distance away. If the Vallejo bikers happened to get suspicious and then find the bug, the two of them would be there to respond.

Yeah, right.

If that happened, they both knew it would probably be too late to help Dexter, but the guy was huge, had brass balls, and could probably kick all their asses anyway.

———————

THAT NIGHT, Game Seven of the Series would be played at Shea Stadium. There had been an East Coast rainstorm on Sunday when Marko was still in Vegas, so the final game of the Series had to be rescheduled. Because of the rain delay, Boston got some additional time to recover from their demoralizing defeat in Game Six. But would it help?

Marko worked late, then wandered over to Harrington's Bar across the street from the ATF office to watch the game. The Red Sox remained in the lead 3-0 after five innings, and things were looking good for Boston. But in the sixth, the Mets finally figured out the pitcher and tied the score. Then, in the bottom of the eighth, Darryl Strawberry homered and it was all over from there.

The world-champion Mets; the defeated Red Sox. All too familiar.

Marko downed the last of his beer. Another dark day for Beantown.

THE NEXT DAY Larry and Marko spent some time with Dexter, setting up the wire and testing it, coaching him on the best way to handle the situation when he was inside. Larry told Dexter to loosen Butch up, get him comfortable and drinking so that maybe he would run on at the mouth about Fort Bragg.

When they cruised past the clubhouse that afternoon, Butch's bike was parked outside. Dexter didn't seem nervous and was willing to go ahead with it. They drove Dexter to where his bike was parked; then they turned back and parked on the clubhouse street.

Dexter pulled up on his bike. For the next hour he was in the clubhouse, all of them drinking, Marko and Larry listening through headphones. As they listened, Dexter finally got around to asking Butch, "Whatever happened to old Billy D?"

From the van, they could hear the room go silent. Nobody

saying a word. The only sound was the tension filling the air. Then Butch suddenly blurted out, "Shit, don't you know anything?"

"Huh?" Dexter said.

They waited through more silence, then heard, "That thieving snitch. He got what he deserved." Marko and Larry looked at each other. It was Butch's voice, no question.

It was a shocking statement, and they'd gotten it on tape. It certainly wasn't an admission of guilt. Far from it. But it tended to establish motive. And if they ever got to the prosecution stage, it was something they could use.

LATER IN THE WEEK, Marko convinced Dexter to go back to the clubhouse. This time, everything went along smoothly until Dexter pushed too hard about Billy Derhammer. Butch was silent at first, but then he got agitated, saying something about smelling a rat.

Marko and Larry both suddenly stood up in the van, Marko cracking his head on the vehicle's roof, thinking they'd have to run in and try to save Dexter. They heard Butch order his buddy Chucky to pull a gun on Dexter. Then they heard the sound of fabric being ripped—probably Dexter's shirt, Marko thought. Butch looking for a wire hidden on Dexter's chest.

Marko impulsively dropped his headphones, reached for the van door to push it open, thinking he would run into the club with his gun drawn. But Larry, who was a little more seasoned, pulled him back. Larry kept listening to the wire, raised his index finger, signaling Marko to wait.

What they heard next was Dexter suddenly go into a

screaming rage. He was shouting obscenities at Butch, Chucky, and the others about accusing him of being a rat and ripping his new shirt.

Academy Award shit, Marko thought.

Except for the torn shirt, Dexter got out of the clubhouse unscathed. The wire in his boot had gone undiscovered, but the damage was done. Marko and Larry retrieved the wire, then debriefed Dexter. They'd gotten the one statement, yes, but they had to concede that another avenue of investigation had now shut down. Dexter told them that it would be a while before he'd be willing to go back in there.

No witnesses, and now no wire. Marko and Larry both knew they were running out of angles.

21

BUTCH HATED FEELING any kind of heat, but lately it seemed like it was coming from every direction. Like the big dumb-looking guy Dexter that Butch had seen hanging around a lot lately. Yeah, well, that's what he was—a hangaround. Butch even kinda liked the guy, but the past couple of times at the clubhouse, Dexter had been getting real nosy, asking too many questions. What was that about? The guy should know better. That business with ripping his shirt, Dexter getting all upset—what did he expect? You're on Cobras property, things happen. You gotta be respectful. No, he wasn't wearing a wire, but that didn't mean he wasn't a snitch. Anybody could be a snitch. It was stupid to take chances. Look what Angel did. Look what Billy Derhammer did.

And then there were those two Feds, Marko-somebody and his partner, snooping around. Assholes. Asking questions to every biker that Butch talked to lately. Even asking his buddies' old ladies. And calling him "Bitch" that day at the house. Those cocksuckers. He wasn't going to forget that.

Butch knew that the Fort Bragg thing had gone way too far,

was almost out of control. Keeping everybody quiet, how long would that last? And not only Angel. But now he didn't even know about her. How could he control her if she wasn't around?

One of the bikers he knew from Vegas had seen her working in a bar, had given Butch a call. If those guys could find her so soon, anybody could. Maybe it was time to leave Vallejo for a while, escape the heat, find Angel in Vegas and let her know that talking to her cop friends wasn't going to work out for her.

Chucky, who'd been with him on the Fort Bragg thing, was leaving town for a while, going over to Bullhead City to stay with an old lady he knew. Bullhead didn't sound too bad. Maybe Butch should head over there, only ninety miles or so from Vegas but a different place entirely. Lots of guys like Chucky around there, doing deals. He'd cruised over to the Vegas area more than once in the past couple of years, liked the ride. But this time he'd take the pickup. He hated to leave his beautiful chopper behind, but it would just be for a week or two. Yeah, take the pickup, be just another good-old-boy on the road. That would be something new.

Besides, Vegas had some real good-looking women. And wouldn't Angel be surprised to see him.

He couldn't wait to see the look on her face.

22

MARNIE KEITH WAS sitting in her office, thinking about Marko Novak, the man she'd met in the bar at the Oakland Airport. It had been over three weeks since they'd exchanged cards after that intense, funny conversation near Gate 8. That day he'd seemed interested in seeing her again—really interested—but she hadn't heard from him. She wasn't accustomed to waiting for men to call. Usually she had the opposite problem. Men falling all over her. At first she wondered if she should call him, make up some excuse for phoning his office. But today he'd finally called to ask her for a date.

Marnie didn't know exactly what it was she liked about Marko. She had only spent a half hour with him, after all. Maybe it was that he seemed like the complete opposite of her ex-husband Edward. Edward was why she was at the airport in the first place. He had been trying to get her back ever since she left the marriage, but now he was putting on real pressure. He'd called to tell her he couldn't live without her, was flying to the Bay Area to see her. Edward, who had everything. Most women would die to be with him. He was rich, educated, successful, good-looking. But he was also older by twenty years, and so controlling.

For almost a year now she'd been single and free, struggling to keep a semblance of the lifestyle she had when she was married to him. Even a good job like hers didn't pay all the bills. She had vowed she would never go back to him, never even get married again. But worrying about money all the time wasn't what she planned on, and at this point, living an easy, secure life had begun to look good again, especially to someone like Marnie, whose mother had been a housemaid.

So there she was, sitting at the bar near Gate 8, waiting for Edward's flight from Las Vegas, ready to have dinner with him at the best restaurant in San Francisco. That night she was all dressed up, saw heads turn as she walked through the terminal in her expensive designer clothes, purchased when she was still married.

And there was Marko—a cute, charming guy who could laugh at himself, wearing sloppy pants and a shapeless old leather jacket, whose drink of choice was brandy and ginger-ale. He looked like he'd been an athlete and made her feel safe the moment he sat down next to her and started talking like they were old friends.

WHEN THEIR FIRST date finally materialized, Marko took Marnie to a little restaurant in Larkspur Landing near the ferry station. Chinese food, but nice, with tablecloths and good food. She could tell he wanted it to be special. Marnie had intentionally dressed down for the date, not expecting much, but she had a great time. Later, when he dropped her off at her

San Rafael condo, she gave him a long good-night kiss.

The second date, two nights later, had been even better, and now she was thinking about him again and, yes, comparing him to Edward.

Marnie knew what money could buy, what it was like to be without it. For her it was all about security. She'd spent almost ten years with Edward—ten years that left her wondering what it would be like to really be in love. But did she even have room for love? She wanted to move up in her job, earn her own way, work on her own terms, but she'd come to it later than most of the women in the company. Regional account coordinator for a leading international cosmetics firm. The chance to go almost anywhere if she was good enough. She had the ambition, and she knew how to be careful. Dressed perfectly for the job, perfect makeup and hair—spending every extra penny on her clothes and her appearance. In her job, you were what you wore and what you had on your face. It wasn't vanity; it was job security. A necessity, if she was going to move up the corporate ladder.

She thought what an odd pair she and Marko would make—Beauty and the Beast. If she wanted to succeed in business, she should be with an elegant man like Edward who could help her with her career.

Yes, that was the way she ought to play it.

But Marko was so much fun.

23

DEXTER CALLED MARKO at the office that morning with some news.

"Yeah, Dexter," Marko said.

"One of my pals told me something I thought you ought'a hear," Dexter said.

"I'm all ears," Marko said, picturing Dexter's huge ears as he said it.

"Butch took off for Vegas."

"When?"

"Yesterday. The guy who told me is a prospect at the Vallejo chapter. Said they're happy to see the back of Butch. Too much shit coming down on them because of him. Chucky Verdugo pulled out too—headed over to Bullhead City."

This news made Marko think that the bikers who Angel mentioned—the ones who'd come into Teddy's Bar—had been there for a reason. What were the odds of a connection between them and Butch's departure for Vegas? Whatever they were, he thought he'd better try to get in touch with Angel.

MARKO AND LARRY were eating lunch at their desks. Marko had ordered a ham-and-cheese sandwich from the corner deli, which was spread out in front of him on a piece of waxed paper next to an extra-large root beer, a bag of chips, and a half-sour pickle. He and Larry were talking sports while they ate, recapping the Series.

When Marko was in Vegas this last time, Larry asked him to put down a hundred-dollar bet on the Red Sox, even though Marko warned him against it. Larry, it seemed, didn't fear the Curse of the Bambino.

Just as Marko entered Caesar's Palace to place the bet, he went to a bank of pay phones to give Larry one last chance to change his mind.

"Don't do it, Larry," Marko said into the phone. "I'm giving you the advice of a lifelong fan here."

"That curse stuff is such bullshit."

"Larry, they haven't won a Series since 1918."

"Well, let's make it a first. Place the bet."

"Okay, but this is one Franklin that's going bye-bye."

Larry was adamant, so Marko went to the betting window with a hundred-dollar bill that, unfortunately, Larry would never see again.

Marko loved sports, loved his Chicago Blackhawks, White Sox, Bears, and Bulls, but didn't mind conversing once in a while about the Red Sox and their perpetual woes. In Vegas, he loved hanging out at sports books, the huge rooms filled with people eating and drinking, the betting windows, the big-screen TVs all showing something different—a game, a race, a fight. He loved how loud they were, hearing the bettors scream when they won. He especially loved the craziness of Sundays during football season, with every game on at once, all the action, always something going on.

Marko's own sports history was long and varied. Wiffle ball on the front porch when he was six, skating in the park near his house, chipping golf balls in the backyard (one exceptionally strong drive blasting through his parents' picture window), batboy duties at Comiskey Park, basketball in the neighbor's rusted hoop; baseball, soccer, and hockey in high school with eight varsity letters; ice hockey in college with one year in the semi-pros.

More than anything, he had wanted to play for the Chicago Blackhawks—a longshot for a Chicago kid—but that dream ended after one year semi-pro with the South Chicago Fire. He was making fifty dollars a game to get his ass kicked, and he quit after one season.

If he couldn't play pro hockey he wanted to be a copper. He wanted excitement and not a boring desk job. He wanted to do the right thing and help people. He wanted a career and a pension. And he never wanted to be laid off, like his father had been. He wanted to retire early and try other things, like finally learning how to play golf.

Marko was a sports nut, a guy fluent in the universal language of guys. He just wanted to be one of the boys.

Marko started telling Larry about last night's date, his second in a week with Marnie Keith.

"I took her to this little Italian joint in San Rafael."

"How was the food?"

"They gave us this little tucked-away booth in the back."

"What'd you eat?" Larry asked.

"I played footsie with her under the table. She loved it."

"They have pizza?" Larry asked.

"And get this—we finish the meal, the waitress comes by with the check, and Marnie picks it up. I say, 'No way,' and grab it out of her hand. I don't know about this woman."

Larry was silent.

"What is it with her, anyway? I've dated, what?—maybe hundreds of women."

"Maybe thousands," Larry said.

"My little black book is stuffed with names—casino waitresses, dealers, bar girls. But Marnie..."

Marko noticed Larry rolling his eyes. He polished off the ham-and-cheese, downed the rest of his soda, looped the can into the trash basket.

Maybe there was something to this love-at-first-sight bullshit.

LAS VEGAS

24

THE SECTION OF Sierra Vista where the pimps and whores lived hadn't seen so many squad cars in almost a year. Angel was on her way home from work, came around the corner, and suddenly confronted the scene on the street—all the Metro cars pulled up in front of the building, their lights flashing, cops coming out of her apartment. She knew right away what had happened. Oh, God, Loretta.

Her next thought was to get away from there as fast as she could.

In the past couple of days, Loretta told her about answering the phone three or four times, someone hanging up. It was Butch, Angel could feel it. He had found her. And now the insane bastard had gotten to her only friend.

Angel walked away as fast as she could, watching her back, no idea of where she would go. Teddy's? No, they'd be watching Teddy's.

She kept walking in the direction she'd come, managed to get all the way to Las Vegas Boulevard, a few blocks south of Tropicana. She found a flea-bag motel, gave the guy at the desk cash, and hunkered down in Room 124. For two nights she stayed there with the chain fastened on the flimsy door, afraid to go out. The TV news blared reports of the attack, but no information on the female victim. Finally, they announced that the woman was in the hospital in critical condition. Loretta was alive! Angel started crying when she heard. God, she wanted to see her, but how was she going to do that? She couldn't even bring herself to leave the motel room.

And where was she supposed to go from here? Angel would never go back to the apartment. Loretta, if she survived, probably wouldn't either. And then there was the matter of money. Angel wouldn't work at Teddy's again. She thought of Marko Novak. He acted like a friend, but he was a cop. She had to remember that. No, she was alone.

How was she going to get away from here? She needed to get to another town, somewhere where Butch wouldn't think to go. Somewhere outside his biker network and all the club-loyalty bullshit. Angel had seen enough of it to make her sick. She wondered if she could somehow barter what she knew for her life. Marko had offered her protection, but she saw that as pretty meaningless. Having to spend the rest of her life in hiding? For what? What had she done?

The motel room reeked of cigarettes, the mattress sagged, the walls were stained from a leak in the roof. She'd been ordering food delivered from the greasy spoon next door. What she wanted to do was go to Teddy's, sit at the big bar, and drink until she fell off the stool. But she was running out of money so she called Marko.

25

RALPHIE, FABIAN MARGULIES' houseboy, opened the door to the big bathroom, holding it just slightly ajar so that the steam wouldn't escape.

"Mr. Fabian, you need to pick up the phone. There's a call from San Francisco, from your friend the cop."

From his bathtub, Fabian asked Ralphie if he could be more specific.

"You know, the big guy, moved away."

Fabian picked up the receiver.

"Fabian, listen to me. This is very important," Marko said. "Angel, the little Hispanic girl who waits tables at Teddy's? The biker's girlfriend I told you about?"

"I remember."

"There was a murder attempt on her roommate, and I'm pretty sure it was meant for Angel. So I need to stash Angel someplace—right now."

"Oh? What about a hotel room?" Fabian said.

"I gotta get her someplace where she'll feel secure. Otherwise, I know she'll run. I need her to turn on Butch

Crowley, and this might make her do it—which won't do me much good if I can't find her."

"You're asking me to be her jailer?"

"Just until I get there."

"When will that be?"

"Tomorrow. I promise."

Fabian was sitting up in the tub, reaching for a towel, thinking fast. Obviously, offering to pay for the hotel wasn't going to work—but friendship, after all, went just so far. Besides, Marko must know that Fabian didn't particularly like having women around the house, not to mention what would happen if this biker-killer who was loose on the streets of Las Vegas came after him, etcetera, etcetera.

"I'll tell her you'll pick her up," Marko said.

"Wait!"

"Fabian, I can't wait. I'm asking for a favor here. Just until tomorrow. Yours is the best place I can think of."

Fabian could, admittedly, see the sense in the arrangement. A big, anonymous house away from the center of town; a good security system.

He grudgingly agreed. "But only for a day or two. Just until you get here. You are going to get here, aren't you?"

"I'll catch a flight tomorrow."

Fabian sent Ralphie to pick up the girl in the Volvo wagon that was used for the grocery shopping. It would give him time to ruminate. Plan his strategy for getting Marko's little angel out of his house.

26

MARKO CALLED ANGEL at the motel, Room 124, told her that a man named Fabian or someone who worked for him would pick her up.

The man pulled up about twenty minutes later, parked in the slot right in front of her room, and knocked on the door.

"Who is it?" Angel said without opening up.

"Ralphie. I work for Mr. Fabian."

Angel cracked the door with the chain still fastened, saw a short, brown, broad-faced man standing there, wearing a white shirt and a tie.

"You ready to go?" Ralphie said. "Can I help you with anything?"

She unfastened the chain, opened the door, scanned the motel's parking lot.

"You got a suitcase I can put in the back?" Ralphie asked.

She'd been wearing the same clothes for three days, brushing her teeth with her finger. She had nothing but her purse and maybe a hundred dollars to her name. Three weeks ago she'd grabbed one small bag to take with her and left everything else at the Vallejo house. Here she was again with nothing.

"No, no suitcase."

He wasn't much taller than she was, and he looked like a Hawaiian or maybe a Samoan. There had been a Hawaiian biker at the Beehive in Oakland, her job when she met Butch. That guy had been twice the size of this one, but the features were similar.

They drove maybe five miles, through Green Valley, finally coming to a house with high walls around it. When Ralphie pushed a button on the dash, the tall iron gate swung open, closing behind them as they drove through.

The house was one story but big, spread out, with lawns and trees all around and a guy working in the yard.

Angel looked over at Ralphie in his crisp white shirt. Suddenly she felt shabby, sitting in the front seat of the big station wagon, like she'd get the place dirty just by being there. The guy worked for Fabian, but he looked rich too. The only time she'd ever felt important or special was riding on the back of Butch's big rumbling Harley, speeding along the highway, wearing her leather jacket, a bandana tied around her head. A biker mama, a Cobras' old lady. But thinking about that scene now made her feel sick to her stomach.

Ralphie parked the car in a gravel enclosure surrounded by clipped shrubs. They went in a side entrance, then down through a long hallway with glass on one wall that faced a pool, lawn on all sides. Angel thought of the crummy little pool at the Sierra Vista apartment building, with its busted pump, the lawn furniture all bent.

How did this Fabian guy get so rich?

She saw him as they passed a high-ceilinged room that looked like an office. He was sitting at a desk, looking over some papers, a big TV across the room showing the news. He was smoking a long cigar and wearing black pajamas with red dragons embroidered on them that reminded Angel of some biker tattoos she'd seen. He looked up from his papers as she stood for a moment in the doorway. When he raised his hand, giving her a little wave, a big chunk of ash fell from the end of the cigar but he didn't seem to notice.

Ralphie led her to a nice little room in a part of the house all by itself, then left her alone.

What now?

She went into the adjoining bathroom, splashed some water on her face, used the nice-smelling soap to wash her hands, looked at herself in the mirror over the sink. Then she lay down on the big bed with its fluffy pillows that matched the pale yellow walls, thinking that Loretta would like this room. Angel thought of all the things her friend had done for her, giving her a place to stay, letting her wear her clothes, use her makeup, getting her in at Teddy's.

How long could she stay here? Could she come and go as she pleased? How long before this guy Fabian threw her out? Then where would she go? It was just weeks since she escaped the prison of being with Butch. Barely escaped. She hoped she hadn't signed up for another. Even Marko's witness protection sounded like another word for prison.

ANGEL FELL SOUNDLY asleep for the first time since Loretta was attacked. When she woke up it was dark, and she wasn't sure where she was. Someone was knocking softly on the door.

"Miss Angel, you awake?"

It was Ralphie's voice on the other side of the door. She'd never been called "Miss Angel" before.

"You want something to eat?"

Angel realized she was famished. When had she eaten? This morning?

"Yeah, okay."

"Dinner's ready in the kitchen. The other end of the hall."

Angel found the kitchen at one end of the long central hallway. Standing at the stove was an older Mexicana, dumpy but with a pretty face, her black hair pulled back into a braid that hung almost to her waist. She was ladling some kind of stew into a bowl over rice. It smelled like something Angel had once eaten in childhood, something her grandmother had made for a special holiday.

"Mr. Fabian has gone out tonight," the woman said. "I'm Juana. I'm the cook."

The kitchen was bright, with a tiny TV on the counter, a big stove with six burners, everything polished. Juana had set a place for Angel at a long kitchen table covered with a bright cloth.

"We ate earlier. Ralphie said you needed to sleep."

Prison? Not like the ones Angel had heard about.

27

BUTCH WAS THINKING that this was the second big mistake in a row. Well, not in a row—there'd been a nice coke deal here in Vegas, which gave him enough cash for a while. That was a good thing, especially because he'd left so much back at the Vallejo house. It was hidden, but still, he was here and it was there.

One of Butch's Vegas biker buddies, where he was staying in a double-wide in the middle of hot-and-dusty nowhere, was the one who'd given Butch a call back in Vallejo. The biker had seen Angel working at a bar called Teddy's on Flamingo Road, had found out that she was living with a dancer named Loretta over on Sierra Vista.

At first, Butch figured he'd just pay Angel a visit, give her a scare like she'd never had before, tell her to keep her mouth shut. But then he realized there was only one way to take care of the Derhammer business once and for all. Not be sentimental about things. So he hired another Vegas biker, a big fat tough dude called Gordo, to go to where Angel was living and take her out. He had shown Gordo a photo-booth picture that Angel gave

Butch when they first got together, back when she was working at the Beehive. Butch thought it looked like her, but not exactly.

Gordo took the job, pocketed Butch's money, said it would be no problem, and then totally fucked it up.

"The bitch in the apartment looked just like Angel," Gordo said.

"Well, you were wrong about that," Butch said.

"You didn't tell me she had a roommate that coulda passed for her sister."

"You should've looked a little harder before you shot her," Butch said.

Butch couldn't believe Gordo would be so stupid. He paid Gordo a good chunk of change to take out Angel, and the asshole hit her roommate by mistake. Not only that, but the roommate, this Loretta, was still breathing, probably already talking to the cops. And Butch knew that when the Vegas cops found Gordo, he'd talk too. He was so dumb, they'd probably trick him into confessing. And then Gordo would take Butch down with him.

"She saw my face," Gordo said.

"Well, you shoulda taken her out, you dumb fuck."

———

GORDO BURST OUT of the double-wide, banging the thin metal door, telling Butch he'd be seeing him around.

Butch thought Gordo must be the stupidest bastard he'd ever come across. And now he was down to it. Now he had to take care of the Gordo mess as well as the rest of it. What should he do? He should head back to Vallejo, get his money and the rest of his stash from the house. Then he'd decide.

He thought about the Fort Bragg mess, how things had gone too far, even with using a safe piece, filing off the serial number, which took forever. And now, if the heat turned on him because of this Gordo thing...

And the Fed, Novak, who was after him like a dog on a scent. Novak would know about Angel being in Vegas. But had Angel talked? Somehow he didn't think so. He knew Angel. She was a yellow bitch. He thought he'd done enough so that she'd keep her mouth shut, but at this point he needed insurance. Maybe getting to her friend would be enough of a warning, but maybe it wouldn't.

If he killed Angel, did the job himself, all roads would lead back to him, and he'd be facing serious time, most likely for the rest of his life. The rest of his life in prison? He'd rather be dead.

But the money. The disrespect. That's what really pissed him off. No-good fucking bitch. Where's my four hundred bucks, Angel?

He twisted the big silver death's-head ring he wore on his left hand, beat his fist against his palm until it ached.

28

EVEN THOUGH MARKO felt like he'd just stepped off the plane in Oakland, there he was again at the airport, heading back to Vegas, except this time the ATF was picking up the tab. The flight on Southwest was forty-nine bucks each way, plus the rental car and hotel room. Whenever he flew to Vegas on his own, he also had to take into account his blackjack money, whatever he won or lost. Would he stay away from the tables this time around? Probably not. He didn't have to work twenty-four hours a day.

Marko promised Fabian that he would get there today, and he didn't want to screw this up. After all the work that he, Larry, and Roy Gorky had done—rounding up the names of the people at the Guerneville rally, over forty interviews by now, getting Dexter to wear the wire, running all the Iron Cobras in Northern California to see if any of them legally possessed a .357 handgun, showing the photo of the slaughtered little girl to every biker old lady they could find—any hope of prosecuting the Derhammer case now appeared to come down to Angel. They needed her, and Marko needed to convince her of that.

But given what she said to him when they talked last week at Teddy's, she wasn't about to testify and go for the witness-protection option. He wondered if the attack on Loretta would change her mind.

———————

MARKO PICKED UP the rental car at McCarran, drove it out to Fabian's place, and found Angel working in the big fancy kitchen. Juana, Fabian's cook, was rolling out pastry on a floured board set out on the marble counter. Angel was wearing a white apron over grey sweats, peeling vegetables. She wasn't wearing a trace of makeup, no big hoop earrings or cheap pendant around her neck; she'd braided her hair so that it hung down her back, like Juana's. She was wearing sneakers. If Marko looked past the older woman's layer of fat, he realized Angel could have passed for Juana's daughter.

From biker tramp to glamorous Vegas cocktail waitress to anonymous-looking domestic in the space of a few weeks. Angel, phase three. Marko was amazed. Maybe she didn't need witness protection. Her latest transformation made her almost unrecognizable.

The thought occurred to him that Angel might be playing the situation in order to remain at Fabian's. She must be terrified to be out on her own, given what happened to Loretta, given that Butch was in town. But she didn't look terrified. She seemed calm. But then the kitchen was a calming place, good smells, everything ordered. Marko felt it too. In fact, Marko thought, everything about Fabian's house was calming. Even the silk pajamas his friend wore around the house.

He tracked Fabian down by the pool.

"I'm glad you thought to get her over here," Fabian said. "Juana likes her, says she's helpful."

"You don't mind?" Marko asked, surprised.

"Not at all. And if you want her to stay here a few more days, that's fine with me."

"Really?" Marko said.

"Marko, you know I like to eat. And Juana is a very, very good cook—so whatever Juana wants…"

ANGEL TOLD MARKO that she wanted to see Loretta, so he worked it out. He called Metro, arranged to visit that afternoon. Loretta was at Sunrise Hospital on Maryland Parkway, where Marko knew a couple of the nurses. He'd met them at a bar called Good Time Charlie's, a happening place right next door to the hospital, where drinks were just fifty cents. All the nurses went there after their shifts.

Angel and Marko left for Sunrise Hospital in the rental car. He'd gotten an update on Loretta's condition from Metro, telling her the news on the way over.

"Listen, Angel, you shouldn't expect much right now. They told me that Loretta wouldn't be able to talk."

"I just want to see her."

"Yeah, well, Loretta's in bad shape," Marko said, "but she just might make it."

"IS SHE SAFE HERE?" Angel asked. They were looking through a glass partition at Loretta, unguarded but seemingly secure in an area that was constantly monitored by the medical staff.

"When she's out of the ICU there'll be a guard at the door to her room."

"What about when she leaves the hospital?"

"We'll get her somewhere safe. I'll talk to Teddy about taking her out to Henderson."

Evidently Loretta had been left for dead by her assailant. Either that, or he was scared off after firing a single shot, which hit Loretta above her left ear and cut her down. Emergency medical technicians had arrived quickly, stabilized her, taken her to Sunrise, about a mile from the apartment building. She still had not regained consciousness. Now, in the ICU, electrode wires snaked from beneath her hospital gown, and intravenous tubes ran down to her arm from a stand of bags. An oxygen mask was over her face, and a patch of hair had been shaved from the left side of her head.

There had been a witness in the apartment complex when Loretta was attacked, a woman who occupied the next apartment, known to Metro as a hooker and a cokehead. She'd been the one to call 9-1-1, a testament to liking Loretta. Not many people in that neighborhood willingly called the cops.

Loretta looked so pale, the blinking, beeping, respiring machines more alive than she was. Hard to imagine her lap dancing in Teddy's back room, shaking her titties for some drunk who'd stuff money in her G-string.

Tits and ass.

Not in the sexless, bloodless ICU.

Angel started crying; Marko put his arm around her shoulder, felt depressed.

29

THE FIRST THING the Metro cops did following the attack on Loretta was interview the next-door neighbor who called 9-1-1.

"My name's Salsa," the women said to the Metro detective who interviewed her at the police substation. She was wearing a blood-red mini-skirt and black patent-leather boots that came up to her thighs. Her blonde curls fell to her shoulders.

"Driver's license says you're Karen Fenster," the detective said.

"Yeah, well, my name's Salsa."

"Okay, Salsa, what happened over there?"

"I heard somebody screaming next door, but I didn't know if it was Loretta or Angel—the girls who live there. Then I heard a gunshot and I called the cops."

"You see the suspect leave the building?"

"I peeked around the front curtain, and I saw this big fat guy running through the yard, around the swimming pool. Next minute I hear sirens. First the cops arrive, then the ambulance people. A few minutes later a cop's pounding on my door. Then a reporter shows up."

The Metro guys who worked the Strip knew Salsa well. She'd been on the game in Vegas for more than a year now, regularly paid security at Dark's Resort and Casino to let her work the rooms. As it happened, the security force at Dark's were the biggest thieves around. They would put the arm on all the working girls for fifty bucks a night, just to let them sit there and be allowed to work. The girls who didn't pay would get tossed. Salsa was a whore but an honest one, not a trick-roll artist or a thief like those Dark's security guys. Whenever anything went down on the Strip, she knew about it.

"The guy looked like he was maybe six feet tall," Salsa told the detective. "Fat Latino guy, but strong-looking. His hair was long, pulled back into a ponytail. Tattoos all over his arms, and one running up the side of his neck. I never seen him before."

At the substation the detective pulled out the mug books and asked Salsa to go through them. After twenty minutes or so of looking, she found two guys who she thought might be the fat tattooed man. One was Ernest Pacheco, who had been arrested for breaking and entering. The other was Roberto Mondragon, also known as "Gordo." Mondragon had a felony assault conviction, for which he'd lived six months at government expense. Metro had last-known addresses for both men and sent out squad cars to find them. The detective told Salsa that when they had the men in custody, they'd get her back to view a line-up.

It was obvious to Metro that this wasn't a professional hit. The shooter had been inept, hadn't even picked up his spent casing. Given that they had Salsa as a witness and also the spent brass, they hoped one of the two men from the mug books would be their guy and it would be quickly resolved.

———————

TWO HOURS LATER, Pacheco was brought into the station. He had an alibi for the time of the attack, working at a convenience store on East Tropicana Road. When they called to check it out, his boss confirmed that he'd been at work, and Pacheco was let go. The address for Roberto Mondragon was no longer current. Metro worked on establishing where he was now living—work records, phone records, utility bills—and came up with a forwarding address. From Mondragon's police record, they also knew that he had biker connections in Vegas.

The next night, Marko got a call at his hotel from his buddy Mike Raleigh, who was a Metro detective. Mike said that the cops had gone to the purported current residence of Mondragon, five miles outside the city in North Las Vegas, warrant in hand.

"No answer at the front door," Mike said. "No answer at the back door, either. Blinds drawn on all the windows."

"They knew it was Gordo's place?" Marko asked.

"The bike and pickup in the garage were registered to him. So they surrounded the house, knocked on the door again. Finally they broke a pane of glass in the back door, unlocked it.

"Turns out, the guy was lying face-up in the middle of the living room. Even with all the blood from the head wound, they could see a thunderbolt tattoo running up the side of his neck."

"Dead?" Marko asked.

"Very," Mike said. "Whoever got him was a lot more careful than Gordo had been at Loretta's place. Nothing obvious left behind—other than the bullet in Gordo's brain."

30

MARKO NEEDED TO get back to San Francisco. The ATF dime that he was living on in Vegas was getting thin, and his main reason for being in Sin City—getting Angel to turn on Butch—was going nowhere. And since he'd arrived there'd been yet another murder. Five and counting.

There was no question in Marko's mind that Butch Crowley was behind the attack on Loretta, that Butch had sent Roberto Mondragon, aka Gordo, to the Sierra Vista apartment to shoot Angel, and that Loretta had been the hapless victim. Marko was also convinced that Butch was responsible for the murder of Gordo. Gordo had been dead only about an hour when Metro found him. Tough luck. If the cops had gotten to Gordo before Butch got to him, then that might have been the key to putting Butch away. But that key was exactly why Gordo was dead.

After the call from Mike, Marko went down to Metro headquarters and spent two hours laying out what he had against Butch to anybody who would listen, trying to convince Mike and the Metro brass to put all their resources behind this case. "...so Butch sees himself as this macho leader of the Vallejo chapter. He doesn't tolerate shit from anybody. Derhammer says, 'Fuck you—me and my tattoo are leaving the club.' Butch says, 'No way, I want that tattoo.' They go up to Fort Bragg, cut off the tattoo, take out Derhammer and his family, who just happen to be home at the time. Sounds insane, but these guys do that kind of shit. Angel Cruz is living with Butch and knows what happened. He terrorizes her so she won't talk, but she leaves town, comes here to Vegas. Butch finds out where she is, hires Mondragon to take her out. Mondragon fucks up, gets Loretta instead. So Butch kills Mondragon to shut him up. That's five people. Five homicides! If you haul in Butch, you'll be hitting the jackpot."

Okay, he'd said it. Marko was glad he'd made the effort. Whatever happened now in Vegas was up to Metro. Tomorrow, he was leaving town.

When Marko thought more about it, he realized that what Butch had created was a reign of terror. Five murders, and the guy was still walking around—no witnesses, no evidence, no means of prosecution. Angel certainly wasn't talking. He could hardly blame her. She saw the bodies pilling up, and she didn't want to be one of them.

That day when Marko saw Butch under the truck at the Vallejo house, he should have taken the shotgun from the Trans Am, blasted Butch into hell where he belonged. But even as he thought this, he also felt that things were beginning to go against Butch. Dexter's report that the Vallejo Cobras were distancing themselves from Butch, that they were sick of the shit he was bringing down on the club, was good news. It convinced Marko that they needed to crank up the pressure back home. Maybe then the biker wall of silence would start to crack.

Tomorrow, when he was back in San Francisco, he had to hit the ground running. In the meantime, he was going to take a little time for himself. He drove over to the Strip, parked the car, walked around for a while. He bought an overpriced shirt in a casino men's store. It was yellow, with a faint gray stripe—not his usual style, but the fabric felt good and he thought Marnie would like it. He went into a gift shop next to the overpriced men's store, looked around for something to get Marnie, settled on a stuffed animal no bigger than his fist. A little pink pig with a rhinestone collar. Expensive. He walked into the casino's coffee shop, sat in a booth, ordered a medium-rare sirloin burger with everything, onion rings on the side. The last time Marko had ordered onion rings he'd been in uniform. When the burger came, he loaded it up. It was juicy, tasty. Other people came into the restaurant, ate their food, left. He didn't care. After the burger, he ordered pie a la mode. He sat there eating, staring at nothing.

Later, back in the hotel room, Marko dialed Marnie's number. Hearing her voice would lift his spirits. All the shit from the past few days, Angel's silence, seeing Loretta lying there barely alive, Gordo's murder—he needed something good to happen.

At least he knew where Angel was and that she was safe.

"Hello, Beautiful," Marko said when Marnie answered the phone.

"Marko. Are you still in Nevada?"

"Yeah. I'm wrapping things up."

"How's it going?"

"Things are always sunny in Vegas," Marko said.

"See you soon, then?"

"I'll be back tomorrow."

"I'll be here."

There was something in her voice. For once, Marko couldn't wait to get home.

31

ANGEL WAS DETERMINED to get back to Sunrise Hospital to see Loretta again as soon as she could. Marko had called her yesterday before he left Vegas for the Bay Area, giving her an update on Loretta's condition.

"She's out of the ICU," Marko said.

"What does that mean?"

"They said she's conscious. She's very weak. Still can't talk."

"I want to see her."

"She's in a private room with a guard at the door. I put your name on the visitors' list. You can see her whenever you want."

That was fine with Angel. At least Loretta was alive. At least Angel could tell her some things she needed to say.

What Marko also passed along to Angel was that Loretta had been shot with a .22 caliber bullet. The bullet was still in Loretta's brain and could be seen on x-ray. It was in an area that didn't threaten her, and the surgeons thought that removing it would be more dangerous than leaving it in place.

That's why they'd kept her in the ICU for so long, and why it had taken her all this time to regain consciousness.

Angel asked Ralphie to drive her the five miles over to the Maryland Parkway facility. When they arrived at Sunrise and she went up to the second floor, the guard outside Loretta's room looked at his list, found Angel's name, checked her ID, and let her inside.

Angel sat down next to the bed, watched her friend, who looked to be asleep. There was a small wound above Loretta's left ear where the hair had been shaved. The size of it surprised her. It didn't seem big enough to have come from a bullet. The edges were smooth, but a ring of red skin circled the tiny hole.

Angel took Loretta's hand, gave it a little squeeze. Loretta opened her eyes, turned her head a fraction in Angel's direction, and smiled weakly. She was still hooked up to machines and an IV, but the oxygen mask was gone, and Loretta no longer looked like she was walking the line between life and death.

Angel knew that if Marko hadn't arranged things, there was no way she could be there with Loretta, no way she could even hear about Loretta's condition. She wasn't on the hospital staff, wasn't a nurse or a doctor, wasn't from the cops, wasn't family.

Angel sat there for a while, not saying anything. It felt good to be silent. She needed to tell Loretta about the guilt she was feeling over the mistaken identity that had almost gotten Loretta killed, but not yet. What she said instead was that she'd heard Loretta was going to be just fine.

"Marko, that ATF guy, arranged for you to stay at Teddy's compound to recover, if that's what you want." Angel felt it would be a good idea for Loretta to stay there. She was thinking about Butch, and also about the goons that Teddy paid to work out there, the ones she'd seen at the pool party. They looked like they could keep anybody away.

"I'm gonna leave town for a while," she said, "but I'll be keeping track of you."

What Angel didn't say was what she intended to tell Marko—that if anything else happened to Loretta, Marko would never hear from her again.

There was something more she didn't tell Loretta—that when Marko told her about Gordo's murder, Angel understood that her chances of staying in Vegas and keeping out of Butch's sights were absolutely zero. Things might be okay as long as she stayed at Fabian's, but she was afraid to leave even for an hour. She was going to get out of Vegas—just head out, leave behind the pretty yellow room, the pool, Juana's kitchen.

Look what happened to you, she thought, looking at Loretta.

Because of me.

NORTHERN CALIFORNIA

32

MARKO COULDN'T HELP listening to the Frank Sinatra lyrics that were floating around in his head. He wanted to fly to the moon, he wanted to play in the stars, and he certainly wanted to know about spring up there on Mars.

He was in the kitchen of his Novato house, a nice space as average kitchens go—well lit, sunny in the mornings, but not particularly well stocked with food. Much of the refrigerator was taken up by beer. He was wearing his pajamas bottoms, his old scuffed slippers, a T-shirt, and a black-and-white Chicago White Sox apron that his sister had sent him for his last birthday. The red potholder next to the stove displayed the Chicago Bulls logo (his other sister). He was putting together what he hoped would be the best omelet he'd ever cooked. This morning it would be cheese, sausage, and mushroom—a Sunday breakfast. Marko Novak, Omelet King. He'd learned his technique from a pro, his former Las Vegas Metro partner Don, who had worked as a kid at an IHOP in Dearborn, Michigan.

It was true Marko's kitchen repertoire was somewhat limited, but he could grill as well as anybody. One of his Vegas girlfriends had once said, "That's what men do—they cook breakfast and they barbeque." Okay with him. Along with pizza and eggs, grilled meat was the stuff of life. The hunter-gatherer-type stuff of life. Hunter? Marko reflected that he loved animals, would never go out and shoot a beautiful elk or a deer. He didn't really even like guns, even though ballistics, as in firearms, was a big part of his ATF job. And he hated shooting the shotgun that was standard equipment for his job because his shoulder would always get black and blue from recoil and hurt for days. As for fishing—hooking worms, and then ripping out the hook and then the guts from innocent fish? He didn't think so. Besides, he was a South Side boy.

Marko cracked another egg into the bowl—for good measure, as his mother used to say. Was this what it felt like to fall in love? This silly, tipsy, floating feeling? Was he hooked, just like one of those poor fish? "Ball and chain," an old expression from his parents' day came to mind. He knew a couple of girls in Vegas who worked as dominatrixes, but that wasn't his thing at all. He probably couldn't even spell it.

Last night in bed, all the stuff from his job just floated away. Finally a night without nightmares. It had been a long time. And this morning it felt like there was a happiness chemical racing around his brain. It felt like he was flying—the sky all blue, a few puffy white clouds floating by—like being in the chopper on those ATF marijuana missions in Mendocino, but without the noise and the violence.

One night in the sack. Did that one night mean the end of other women? Was he really going to trade all those women for just one? Was that fair? All those dates he'd been on... years of them. Yes, it had been fun—a lot of fun. But it had also been a kind of quest, accumulating the finest black book he'd ever seen.

And now, one woman? He didn't know if Marnie was the me-and-only-me type. And it's not like she was making any demands on him. One night, after all. Maybe she was even seeing other guys. Shit, that was a depressing thought. But maybe what Marko wanted was her-and-only-her.

He heard the bathroom door open, watched as Marnie floated into the kitchen, wearing the top half of his pajamas. Her beautiful dark hair brushed her shoulders, those lovely long legs showing beneath the pajama top. Any thoughts of other women flew out of his mind. He tried to be cool but couldn't help himself. He reached over and turned off the burner. He led her back to the bedroom.

They'd eat later.

33

ON THE DRIVE from Vegas back to Vallejo, Butch's old blue pickup was threatening to leave him stranded under some cactus in the middle of the desert. He thought about driving up through Reno, then straight over on 80, but the pickup turned him against that route. Instead, he headed southwest into the Mohave, over to Barstow and Bakersfield. From there he would take 5 North to the Bay Area.

Butch didn't normally take much time to think, especially when he was driving. Usually the rumble of the chopper, the sound of the wind, the feeling of being carried along by the great machine totally occupied his mind. No space for thinking about things. And when he was in the pickup, he'd turn on the radio; turn it up loud. But this time, driving across the desert, there were long stretches where all he heard were the Mexican stations, or maybe some preacher, so instead he spent the time thinking about things.

Driving through the endless Mohave he thought about the limp he still had from the beating his father gave him when he was a kid. With him all these years. Butch was only six, couldn't fight back. But he learned how. He definitely learned how. Now he could kick the shit out of his father, give him what he deserved—if he'd still been around.

Near Barstow, Butch thought about the time he stabbed his high-school teacher with the point of a compass. It meant the end of school, but the bitch deserved it. As far as he was concerned it was the best thing that could have happened. Butch educated himself after that.

Then near Boron, in Antelope Valley, north of Edwards airbase, he thought about the military. Those flat dry lakebeds that they used as runways—he knew about the rocket tests, the early supersonic flights, the speed and altitude records, the Space Shuttle. When he was a teenager, he thought the military might be his escape but was sure they wouldn't take him because of his limp.

At Tehachapi, in the mountains, near the state prison—a serious one here, maximum security—he thought about all the guys he knew in stir; near Bakersfield, about the shitty factory job he had a few years back. Janitor on the night shift. Yeah, he really would have gone someplace with that one. That was before he joined the Cobras and got into selling guns and dope and whatever else would help him build up his well-hidden stash in Vallejo.

Then he thought of his Vallejo buddies—his ex-buddies, who these days seemed to think that Butch was the source of their trouble. Scumbags. About Angel, her leaving, her stealing. About Billy and how his disrespect had gotten Butch into all the current shit. Billy who disrespected Butch's orders—that the Cobras tattoo had to be burned off. Billy instead adding the "out 1986"—no good, and Billy knew it. And now, all this shit. After getting to Derhammer's Fort Bragg place so late, with the kids home, the wife screaming. He'd never intended to kill the whole family, never intended to kill anyone, but that's what went down. All the blood, blood even covering his favorite jeans. Then back to Vallejo, home, Angel there, seeing him.

And now. Her gone. Chucky Verdugo gone to Bullhead City, Charley Mapes back to Detroit, Johnny LaSalle—he didn't know where Johnny was. Then all the Vegas bullshit. Angel, Loretta, Gordo. It made his head ache.

―――――――

THE VALLEJO HOUSE was dark and uninhabited when Butch finally arrived. He was exhausted from driving, mostly from thinking. He unlocked the garage door, opened it, and backed the truck inside. He gave his bike a once-over before closing the garage behind him and heading to the house.

As he was unlocking the back door—the lock in the knob, the two dead bolts—he had to admit that he was glad to be back. He pushed open the door to the dark house, but something was blocking it. He reached in for the light switch, flipped on the light. It wasn't *something*, it was lots of things. He pushed his way inside, saw what it was. It was all the things in the kitchen. Everything strewn across the floor, drawers pulled out, turned out, empty. Plates, glasses, and pans. Cereal boxes, food containers, all emptied onto the floor or the counters.

He went into the front room, turned on the light. The room was completely trashed. The couch cushions were ripped open, the recliner was on its side, its upholstery ripped off the frame. The big TV was smashed.

In both bedrooms it was the same. Every piece of clothing,

everything that hung in the closets—thrown on the floor; cardboard boxes filled with worthless shit were tossed and emptied. Mattresses slashed.

He stood there and stared. They—whoever they were—had done a job.

The question was, had they found what they were looking for?

He headed for the bathroom. No sign of anything much here—not much damage. The medicine cabinet was empty, things pushed out onto the sink. For a split second he was thankful to Angel. When she left with his four hundred bucks, he spent a couple of hours sweeping the house clean of anything else that could be easily found. Not a single dime in sight. Not any kind of stash.

Now, though, there was the secret place.

He went back to the kitchen, to the back door, kicked away some shit on the floor, closed the door tight and relocked it. He found two screwdrivers—a Phillips-head and a flat-head—on the floor in the kitchen, in a pile of random tools dumped out from a drawer. Brought them back to the bathroom. He pulled out the stuff that was still under the sink—a roll of toilet paper, an open pack of Q-tips, a bottle of red cough medicine on its side, leaking. He unscrewed the bottom of the cabinet, four screws holding it down. Then he pried up the junky piece of dark-brown wood. Beneath it there was some quarry tile, just like on the bathroom floor, but here ungrouted. No sign of anything disturbed. He took up the tile. Underneath the tile was the sub floor, with a cutout. He raised the thick rectangle of plywood subflooring with the flat screwdriver, reached inside the hole.

It was there.

When he felt it, a wave of relief flooded his body. A box the size of a small shoebox, but plastic, with a tight-fitting lid, sealed with layers of duct tape. He almost left it where it was, but thought no, look inside. Just for peace of mind. It was hard to pull the box through the opening, barely big enough for the box itself, but he angled it through the hole. Leaving the box on the sink, he went back to the kitchen for the box cutter that had been lying on the floor near the screwdrivers.

Butch shoved the blade up the throat of the tool, marched back through the random violence left over from the futile search.

So fucking what.

Nothing in the whole goddamn house mattered but the box. He leaned on the edge of the sink while he cut away the tape, carefully. This and his bike, what he possessed. Finally, he lifted the lid, still tacky from the duct tape.

When he reached into it, his hand felt a thick wad. Good. Butch pulled it out. All his money—the fat bag of coke. Everything. He looked at it.

No.

It wasn't that anymore. Now what he held in his hand was a thick wad of newspaper.

It was then that he started screaming. He didn't stop. He didn't know how long it lasted or care if they heard him a mile away.

Finally he slumped down onto the bathroom floor.

What was it—two, three years' work?

Gone.

Butch screamed again, but this time it was more like a

moan, the sound going on inside his head but not coming out of his mouth. To him, it was loud enough to burst his ears.

That night he slept on the ruined mattress, dragging it onto the floor and piling blankets on top of the gashes so that he wouldn't feel them. If it had been just a couple of weeks ago, he could have gone to the clubhouse, slept on the couch, but the welcome mat wasn't out right now. If anyone came after him tonight, they'd better say their prayers.

What filled him? Rage, or fear? He didn't have a word for it, but lying there on the ruined mattress, it was something so full that it took over his whole body. There was no chance for sleep. Sleep was an afterthought. Waves of it coursed through him. He couldn't stop them. It was like his body was electrified by it. Tingling with it.

34

EVEN THOUGH THE relationship still felt new, Marnie was starting to get used to Marko Novak. But being with a man in law enforcement, someone who regularly packed a revolver in an ankle holster, wasn't always easy.

She and Marko were spending more and more time together, which she liked. But then there was the other stuff, new things that she'd never had to deal with before.

First, the sleeping together. Yes, the sex was great. A new kind of sex for her—deep, so pleasurable. But the sleeping part—that meant sleeping with a man who lived his job in his dreams, who tossed in his sleep, mumbled, bolted awake in a sweat. Some night his legs would jerk, almost like he was running. One night he woke up crying.

Every night another nightmare. Every night, when he wasn't looking, a drama played out in front of her.

The nightmares were the only way she knew that he was really up against something. All he would tell her about that part of his job was that he had to be smart and careful.

Whenever they went to a restaurant or a bar, it was always

the same routine. He'd sit with his back to the wall.

"Marko, is something wrong?" she asked him one time. "You keep looking around the room."

"I'm just checking things out."

"What things?"

"Well, I just want us to be safe."

"We are safe; we've come here twice this week."

Even when it seemed that he was thinking only of her, she realized he knew everything that was going on in the room. It was as though another dialog was going on, and she was left out of it. And then there was the secrecy, not telling anyone who he was or where he worked.

The nights they slept together, he liked it better when they stayed at his house, where he kept his Smith and Wesson five-shot Detective Special in the nightstand next to the bed.

Weeknights when Marnie slept over, she'd have to get up at six-thirty in order to get to work in the city by nine. She started leaving a toothbrush and a few cosmetics in the bathroom, and some things in his closet, right there next to his junky clothes. That was another issue—the junky clothes. Marnie could hardly bear to see what Marko was going to put on in the morning.

One day she bought him a beautiful silk tie. She was hoping it would replace the two permanently food-stained ones hanging in his closet. Not that you could really see the stains through the loud patterns. The best of the two was pinkish-red, with depictions of various fruits—bananas, watermelon, grapes—his Carmen Miranda tie.

"It's for when you go to court," Marnie said as he opened the long flat box.

"Nice."

"I noticed that the ties in your closet are stained."

"That's why I buy ones with patterns."

"So the stains won't show?"

"Well, yeah..." Marko said, looking a bit hurt.

He wore the new silk tie the following week for a court date, but like a nice new chair brought into a shabby room, it made the clothes he was wearing look even junkier.

Then they went to the wedding of one of her friends. Marko wore a polyester suit, and Marnie decided to step in.

"Marko, I think we should go shopping."

"Shopping?"

"For some clothes."

"Your clothes are terrific," Marko said.

"For you."

"Oh."

"It'll be good for your career," Marnie said.

"It will?"

"Sure. You get more respect when you wear good clothes. Besides, the department stores where I do business give me discounts. Big discounts."

But it wasn't just for him. How was she supposed to climb the ladder of a cosmetics corporation with a man who wore polyester suits?

One day after they went shopping, Marko starting wearing a nice jacket and slacks to work and things changed. Suddenly, he liked the attention he got from dressing well. Suddenly, he was more self-assured. Marnie knew the change would help both of them, if they ever got to the point where she could take him out with her colleagues.

For now, when they went out, a bar was pretty much where they would go. That's where his friends were. If she wanted to be with him, it was going to be in a bar. Eventually it was going to affect her career, she knew it. Maybe not this week, maybe not even this month, but someday it would.

Which brought up the drinking issue. All the agents drank too much. And Marko was right up there, hitting it hard, but she knew he did it partly to forget about the things he saw in his job. And now that she was with Marko, she drank too much. Too much, at least, for the demanding job that she had.

Next on her list was what she called his dumb-blond complex. His record of womanizing. The bar girls, waitresses, dancers... the shallower the better, the sleazier the better. She figured that before she stepped into the picture, he'd only wanted to worry about himself, not a wife. It fit with the job.

One thing that came from Marko's womanizing, she had to admit, was that he was good in bed. Edward had been an indifferent lover; his power lay elsewhere—in wealth and success, and the confidence that went with it.

As to Marko, even though they were still at the beginning, she was dealing with a very long list. She tried not to be daunted by it. Who knew? Through it all there was the wonderful sense of humor, the way he could laugh at himself.

She hoped the problems would just go away by themselves, or that she'd get sick of the comparison game. Maybe she should turn it into a two-column list—Edward on one side, Marko on the other. What was the cost, what was the payoff? The thought made her feel like she was taking a test. Who would win? Marnie couldn't begin to guess, and she didn't want to outsmart herself.

35

IT WAS EARLY, not even six-thirty, two days after Butch had gotten back to Vallejo. He hadn't bothered to eat anything this morning other than a couple of Dunkin' Donuts he'd picked up on the way over. He was sitting in the blue pickup, his leather jacket zipped up against the cool weather, down the block from Marko Novak's house in Novato, watching, waiting for an idea to come to him.

He spent that first night, lying there on the trashed mattress, and all day yesterday thinking about what to do. He had calmed down from that night, when the rage he felt made his body seem like it was going to explode. What he figured was that somehow the cops or the Feds were connected to the missing money. Who else could it be? No question they were trying to get to him. First, they made all his buddies paranoid about being around him. That's what the clubhouse rebuff was all about. Then they tried to cut off his options by stealing his cash, his stash. Okay. He got the plan. And now there would be some justice. His whole body could feel it. He was aching for retribution.

Isn't that why Butch and the Iron Cobras were such a perfect fit? Justice when justice was due? Somebody says the wrong thing to a brother, steals from a brother—don't fuck with me, don't fuck with my buddies. They were a team. There should be a Cobras for kids, he thought, so Dad would have to think twice before kicking the shit out of his six-year-old boy, leaving him limping for the rest of his life.

This time, though, Butch was alone.

He needed to do this one thing, then he'd leave town. He decided that when he left it would be on the bike. He wasn't going to leave it behind. If he needed a car he could steal one. He knew he could make money the Iron Cobras way, wherever he was. But if it came down to it, there was always the bike, worth thousands.

This was the second morning in a row that he'd been here watching Novak's house, and it was the second time he'd seen the good-looking woman leave. Novak stood at the front door, kissing her. The bitch got into her car, started it up—the exhaust showing in the damp morning air—and headed out. This was his chance. This time Butch followed.

She was driving a red Honda Prelude, heading south. Butch wondered if she was on her way to work, but he didn't think so from the way she was dressed. Jeans. Novak and the woman were early risers, because it was still a while before rush hour. She was taking the side roads, and there wasn't much traffic, but enough so that Butch could keep a few cars between them.

A dozen miles south, they were in San Rafael, driving through the town, then along the side streets. Butch didn't have a clue where they were headed. Eventually she turned into a driveway that led to a set of low buildings—he guessed they were apartments or condos—set back from the road and bordered on two sides by trees. He didn't follow her in but saw that she was pulling up near the last building, parking the red car in a space under a metal roof, then getting out and walking to the building. When she was inside, he pulled slowly into the lot. He parked the pickup a few slots down from her car in one of the empty numbered spaces.

Butch waited, deciding what he would do, telling himself not to make any mistakes, to think of some consequences for once.

Fuck the consequences.

No, don't fuck the consequences.

Remember all this shit started with Fort Bragg.

He went back and forth, back and forth about it. If he got the chance, and sooner or later he would—nobody around, not many cars, not a single person in the time he'd been sitting there—he figured he'd make it look like a mugging. Let them guess what it was really about. Then he'd be on his way.

He thought this building was probably where she lived. Maybe she'd be leaving again for work. And a dozen minutes later there she was, coming out the door, all dressed up, made up, wearing high heels.

Butch grinned. He knew what high heels were for—and they weren't for running away. She was carrying a black purse and a big white plastic bag, heading for the dumpster at the back of the lot. The dumpster was hidden away in a little enclosure, so that nobody who lived there would have to be reminded of garbage. Perfect. He suddenly felt invincible. If he thought about it, he would have known the feeling was adrenaline, but at that moment he felt too high to think.

He'd have to be quick. He picked up the stocking beside him on the seat, pulled up the collar of his jacket, and, looking around, trailed her to the enclosure.

It was time for some payback.

36

THIS THING MARKO was having with Marnie—what was he supposed to call it? this love thing—it was actually starting to work out. They could be together, go out and have fun, make love whenever they wanted, sleep together all night, and both get to work, no problem. It was easy.

Usually they left the house at the same time, but this morning Marnie took off before he did. She needed to stop off at her condo in San Rafael before going to work. They'd been up early, had some coffee, sat around in the kitchen for a few minutes in their pajamas—actually, his pajamas. The sun was starting to come into the big kitchen window, and the room was warm. It felt cozy. Almost as intimate as lying together in bed. Marko made toast, put butter and a jar of jam on the table, and they ate a bit of breakfast. Then Marnie got dressed. She kissed him good-bye as they stood on the front step, and took off in her little red Honda. He left for work not long afterward.

––––––––––

WHEN HE GOT to the ATF office an hour later, one of the

messages on his desk said to call Fabian Margulies. Oh, shit. Was it about Angel? Was she all right? Had Butch somehow gotten to her?

He dialed Fabian's Vegas number.

"She took off, Marko," Fabian said. "Not a word to any of us."

"Just like that? No note or anything?"

"Nothing. She must have left early this morning. Ralphie says her things are gone—not that she had much."

"Goddammit," Marko said, feeling his depression creep out of its cave.

"I feel bad about this," Fabian said.

"Not your fault."

"Still..."

"It wasn't your job to keep her there."

"Well, we liked her. Juana is quite upset..."

"I'll let Metro know she's gone."

Marko called his buddy Mike Raleigh at Vegas Metro, told him Angel had fled.

"You're not exactly on a roll with this one, are you," Mike said.

"You got anything more on the Gordo killing," Marko asked.

"Still a dead end. As far as we're concerned, it's just one gang-banger shooting another. Makes our job easier when they do it to themselves."

Marko said he'd stay in touch, replaced the receiver, then banged his fist on the desk loud enough that Larry wandered over.

"Why didn't I keep on top of it? At the very least I should have called her every day."

"Can't think of everything," Larry said. "It might not have made any difference."

"Our only witness. How could she do it?"

MARKO LEFT THE OFFICE, went out to meet Gorky. When he saw him, he'd have to deliver the latest news about Angel. Gorky was going to be upset.

An hour later, on his way to Ukiah, Marko's pager went off. He found a pay phone, put in a call to Larry.

Larry sounded hesitant. "Uh, it's about Marnie..."

"Marnie?" Marko froze when he heard her name.

"A detective from San Rafael PD called. Said she was mugged."

"What happened? Is she okay?"

"They got her purse. But she was beat up pretty bad."

"Beat up? Where is she?"

"Kaiser Hospital in San Rafael.

Marko thought for a moment, said, "Larry, you know what this is about."

"Maybe..." Larry said.

Marko got back in the car, headed south, his thoughts racing faster than his government car could get him to the hospital.

WHEN HE GOT to Kaiser, they were still working on Marnie. The detective from the San Rafael PD found him in the waiting room, and they went to the lunchroom to talk.

"A mugging?" Marko said. "Did she get a look at him?"

"Guy was wearing a stocking over his head."

The detective went through the information that they had—time of attack, response by the PD, condition of the victim.

"She fought back hard," he told Marko. "Luckily, somebody from the apartment complex came by. Somebody else shouted at the perp and then called us. It could have been worse."

"Can the witnesses ID him?"

"Same problem with the stocking. But both Marnie and the witnesses thought the guy had a little black beard."

Butch's goatee.

Marko debated how much to tell the detective. He was thinking about the two-plus hours that he'd spent with Vegas Metro after the murder of Gordo, trying to convince them of Butch's sadistic spree.

He told the San Rafael cop that he'd been working on a case involving some motorcycle outlaws and was considering whether this was more likely a revenge thing. It was an ongoing case—Mendocino sheriff's department, the ATF.

He and the San Rafael cop agreed to keep each other informed.

Marko found a phone and gave Larry a call.

"Do you believe this fucking coward, going after Marnie? Why didn't he just come after me?" Marko said. "We gotta find him."

"I'll drive over to the Vallejo house," Larry said, "see if I see anything."

"I'll be at Kaiser. I'll let you know when I find out what the scumbag did to Marnie. Maybe she can give me more of an ID."

Marko sat in the waiting room. Part of him hoped this

really was a random mugging and not Butch. That was something he could deal with. If it was Butch, then the attack on Marnie—well, it really came down to his own carelessness and stupidity, didn't it. Allowing a slimeball like Butch to tail him home, and then go after his girlfriend?

How much dumber could Marko get?

37

BRUISED KIDNEYS, a broken nose, two broken ribs—that's what the doctor reported to Marko. Marnie's injuries were bad enough that she had to spend two days in the hospital and be sedated to numb the pain. Marko camped out in her room, wanting to help, even in some small way.

The second day of her hospital stay, Edward arrived carrying a huge bouquet of flowers. Marko had heard about Marnie's ex-husband, but this was the first time he'd seen him. He had to admit that the older man was impressive, everything that Marko was not—wealthy, educated, with ten years of marriage to Marnie. Jealousy, the green dragon, entered the room and sat there breathing some fire down Marko's neck.

Marnie had mentioned Edward from time to time. Not in an obnoxious way—nothing Marnie did was obnoxious—but just to let Marko know that it wasn't necessarily clear sailing into the sunset for her and Marko.

One night, after they'd had a few drinks, Marko had gotten Marnie to admit that Edward still loved her, still wanted her. In that equation, it was Marko who came out on top. Maybe it was

Edward who was envying *him*, wondering what made him the man that Marnie chose to spend her time with.

What had Marnie said about Edward? She said she'd found him too controlling. Okay, that much he understood. But as Marko talked to the man, saw his easy charm, his good looks, he wondered, frankly, why she'd given up on the marriage. Despite all his past girlfriends, Marko knew he would never really understand women, what they were about, what they wanted.

He sometimes fantasized about what it would be like to give Marnie everything she needed, to fit in with the glamorous life around her job and her ambitions. Usually he would just declare himself hopelessly blue collar and be satisfied with that. Mr. Tough Guy from the South Side. Take it or leave it. He wasn't magically going to become a rich somebody with an Ivy League education, one of the people who naturally ruled the world.

But it would be nice to be everything Marnie wanted. Especially nice if he didn't have to change much about himself. Actually, he would change some things for her; he felt it more every time he was with her.

Instead, what had he done? Been responsible for Marnie being attacked. That was a tough burden to carry. He wondered if Edward knew, if Edward was blaming Marko for what had happened to the woman he still loved?

Yesterday, when Marko had first seen her, her face all bruised, black eyes, the stitches, she'd said, "You're not responsible for what other people do." She had slurred her words a bit, from the painkillers, but hearing her say that had helped Marko a lot.

But this stuff about Edward was just about Edward. The

important thing here was Marnie. What Edward did for Marko was make him realize how valuable Marnie was. Precious? He didn't dare use that word. That meant just about irreplaceable. He was too young for that. Almost all of his life was ahead of him, full of options. Maybe full of other women. If Marnie left him, eventually there would be someone else. Regret—that was the thing to avoid. It was the worst feeling, worse than guilt. The point was to do the right thing in the first place. And if coming from the streets of Chicago made him not always know what that was—in Marnie's terms—then that's the way it was going to be.

The fall from Marnie's arms, if it happened, would be far. He'd started to think of himself differently in the past couple of months, that he could be something more than he'd been before. That was because of Marnie.

Scenario: Girlfriend gets beaten up because cop-boyfriend fails to stop the vicious punk who's already killed five people. Rich ex-husband is waiting in the wings to pick up the pieces, hoping to get his beautiful wife back.

Marko knew he hadn't seen that one on the silver screen. Throw in the Vegas stuff, the biker stuff, maybe something about the cosmetics industry, mean streets of Chicago...

Marko Novak, screenwriter. Maybe someday. In the meantime, he was living at least part of it. He just wished they could all move on to the next scene.

THREE WEEKS LATER

38

THREE WEEKS AND counting since the attack outside her condo, and Marnie was healing and back at work. The black and blue had disappeared from around her eyes, and, thanks to an expert doctor, her nose looked the same as it had before the attack. Initially, the doctor had put packing in her nostrils, then taped her nose, the tape remaining in place for over a week. Now it was nearly her same old nose.

"What about my nose?" she said to Marko. "Don't you think it looks different?"

"It's beautiful," Marko said, wanting to kiss the tip of it.

The kidney bruising had left her feeling fragile and sore. At first she didn't want to move, didn't want to get out of bed. But that was mostly resolved.

"Ouch," Marnie said, when Marko absent-mindedly put his arms around her. Even though her ribs were giving her less pain, it was no good when he tried to hold her. She couldn't wear tape on the fragile skin there, so it was a matter of waiting for the bones to knit.

Right after the attack she'd been sedated, then the doctor

prescribed a heavy dose of painkillers. She had backed off the drugs but still took them on a fairly regular basis. It was the only way she could function, especially in her first days back at work.

Marnie told Marko that she didn't yet have the energy for a social life, and they spent less time together than before the attack. When they were together, it was mostly at her place. Marko was solicitous, bringing flowers and little gifts when he came by, and always showing up with some groceries, cooking things she liked, like chicken and fish, things a committed carnivore wouldn't make for himself. He did everything he could think of to try and make it up to her.

Wasn't this exactly why he had avoided a real involvement for so long? So he wouldn't have feelings like this? Every time he saw Marnie, it brought up the guilt—the endless frustration of the Derhammer case, along with his anger that she had been a victim of it, and that Butch was still free to walk around.

Marko was missing the kind of time he and Marnie had together before the attack, the sex, the fun, the hanging out. He missed being able to hug her and kiss her. He wanted her to want him physically the way she had before, to go out drinking with their friends—with his friends, actually. They were his buddies, he realized. That's one part of the relationship he'd have to think more about, maybe change something.

Whenever they saw each other, he wore the new clothes they'd bought together. He liked them well enough, but he wore them because she liked to see him looking good. She didn't want to drink, so he drank only a beer or two around her, nothing more. It was a change. Drinking made everything go smoother, and it wasn't easy for him to cut down.

He wanted her to heal and be strong again. He wanted things to be normal. Mostly, he wanted it to be the way it was before.

––––––––

ROY GORKY WAS the one who was really suffering. He'd made that promise to Trudy Peck—that he wouldn't rest until he caught the bastards who killed her sister and her family. Gorky had taken it literally, and it plagued him. He was a stand-up cop who took the job of doing right by society very personally. He'd been on the wagon for years, but Marko heard that he had fallen off, hitting it pretty hard. One night, after a bout of heavy drinking, Roy fell asleep in his car in the parking lot of a tavern. His wife was frantic. She knew that Marko and Roy had gotten friendly, and the next day she called Marko to talk about the parking-lot sleepover.

"I was worried sick, Marko."

"He getting any help?" Marko asked.

"I begged him to go to AA."

"And?"

"He went twice."

"Only twice?"

"It didn't work out. He says it's not his thing."

Marko understood. He knew others who'd tried that route and given up.

"It keeps getting worse," she said. "I feel like the only thing I can do is leave for a while."

Which would kill Gorky, Marko thought.

A few days after the talk with Gorky's wife, Marko got another call from Mendocino. This time it was Roy himself. The two hadn't spoken since the attack on Marnie, and when Gorky greeted him, Marko felt remiss, thinking of the detective's current problems with drinking, until he heard the excitement in his voice.

Roy had just gotten a call from the Detroit DEA, from a special agent named Raymond Jarvis.

"Marko, you ain't gonna believe this... DEA's got some punk locked up on fourteen keys who wants to rat. Claims he was at the Fort Bragg farmhouse that night."

"Get outta here..." Marko said.

"Yes, sir."

"Holy shit."

"Baby, we gotta get ourselves to Motown!"

DETROIT

39

IT WAS A FROSTY, early-spring day at Windsor Crossing in the province of Ontario, the busiest border crossing between Canada and the United States. The two men sat in their white panel van, the radio turned low, the van's heater making the atmosphere close. They were waiting for their turn at the Customs station, watching the drug-detection canines and their handlers approach several vehicles to their left. Then the handlers headed toward the white van. When the dogs circled them, then moved off toward other vehicles, both men breathed a sigh of relief. A minute later their turn came to pull up to the Customs window.

"What's in the van?" the official asked them.

"Plants and some dirt," the driver said.

"Where are you headed?"

"Just to Detroit and back."

The official waved the van through, and they drove off. As they passed the sign that read Welcome to the USA, the two men exchanged a high-five. Home free. The driver lit a cigarette, reached over to turn up the music. It was Creedence doing "Bad

Moon Rising." Swamp rock. The music made it seem like summer was just around the corner. The driver started singing along, singing about a bad moon rising and how trouble was on the way.... It was time to breathe again.

But not for long.

Before the driver even got to the chorus, a caravan of squad cars and unmarked law-enforcement vehicles pulled out. They surrounded the van and pulled it over. Less than a minute later, the thwap, thwap, thwap of a police helicopter sounded overhead, hovering. The whole event looked like it was choreographed, some kind of vehicular ballet.

The two men were ordered out of the van, handcuffed, and escorted to the front of a Detroit Police Department squad car. As the arrest proceeded, Canadian Customs officials and the Royal Canadian Mounted Police watched from the bridge, a hundred and fifty feet above the Detroit River. Their international plan of law enforcement was working perfectly.

Special Agent Raymond Jarvis, an extremely tall, almost gawky DEA agent, went to the trunk of his unmarked vehicle and pulled out a power saw. He carried it over to the unoccupied van, engaged the saw's motor with a loud buzz, started cutting the floorboard in the back of the van. Everyone stood by to watch. Jarvis's confidential informant said the drugs would be hidden there, and the agent just happened to have a search warrant in his back pocket. It was signed by the US magistrate.

After a few noisy minutes with the power saw, Jarvis yelled "Bingo!" He emerged holding up a package wrapped in plastic.

Seeing what the DEA man had found, the van driver and his passenger hung their heads. The van was seized and towed, and the suspects were taken to be processed in the federal system.

An hour later, the report came in. When it was all accounted for, the van contained fourteen kilos of cocaine.

———————

AT THE DETROIT DEA office, the two men were separated and placed in holding cells. Agent Jarvis gave the driver the first crack at helping himself. His California driver's license identified him as Charles Harvey Mapes.

"You need to give up the source of the drugs, Mapes."

Mapes said nothing, and Jarvis repeated the demand.

"I'm just the driver," Mapes said. "I don't know anything about this shit."

Yeah, sure. Jarvis continued the interrogation, but when it became obvious that Mapes wasn't going to cooperate, the agent decided to leave him sitting alone for half an hour.

As he shut the cell door behind him, Jarvis said, "Fourteen kilos should get you some serious time—say, twenty years?"

Next was the passenger, identified as Richard "Check" Chesnutt, with a Florida driver's license. He claimed he was just along for the ride, and he too refused to cooperate.

Jarvis let them both stew for a while, but when he went back to Mapes's cell, he still got nothing from the driver. Jarvis had seen a lot of punks, and Mapes seemed like the kind of punk who knew how the game was played. For sure he'd spent the time alone thinking about how to save his ass.

Finally Jarvis said, "Okay. You got one last chance here. What's it gonna be?"

Mapes said, "How 'bout I give you a homicide?"

"What kind of homicide?"

"A quadruple homicide."

Jarvis rolled his eyes. He'd heard it before. "Where and when did this take place?"

"It was in Mendocino County—Fort Bragg, California."

"When?"

"October 6, 1986."

"How do you know about it?"

"Let's just say I was there."

Jarvis didn't know if there was a town called Fort Bragg in California, or even a county named Mendocino. He went to the desk, put in a call to his DEA office in San Francisco to get the lay of the land.

When he found out about Fort Bragg and last fall's homicides, that's when he dialed the Mendocino County Sheriff's Office, was put through to Detective Roy Gorky, and gave him the news about their captive songbird.

40

A FEW HOURS after DEA Agent Raymond Jarvis phoned the Mendocino County Sheriff's office, Marko and Gorky drove to the San Francisco airport and boarded a late flight to Detroit. Gorky was high from the news of a possible break in the Derhammer case. All during the flight, he acted like a nerdy adolescent who had just been kissed by a popular girl. Every few minutes he would elbow Marko and say, "I can't believe it. I just can't believe it."

Each time Gorky said it, Marko, the ex-Vegas cop, thought, Yeah, well, if it sounds too good to be true... But even he had to admit that getting a break like this, totally from left field, would be pretty amazing if it worked out.

When they landed in Detroit, it was too late to do anything but go to the hotel and catch some sleep. First thing the next morning, they arrived at the Detroit DEA office, where Jarvis agreed to set up an interview with Mapes.

Gorky read Charles Mapes his rights. Mapes told them he understood and that he wanted to talk.

"Look, I was only the driver that night. I didn't hurt

anybody, I didn't kill anybody, and I didn't set the fire."

Marko and Gorky just smiled.

"Billy Derhammer was treasurer of the Vallejo Cobras," he said. "Butch Crowley accused Billy of stealing money, and he also thought maybe Billy was a snitch. So Butch and Chucky Verdugo forced Billy out of the club, which meant that Billy had to turn in his colors and get rid of his tattoo."

"Get rid of it?" Marko said. "How?"

"Burn it off, or shave it off. It was a club rule—only Iron Cobras can have a Cobras tattoo. If a Cobra leaves in bad standing, the tattoo comes off. But instead Billy tattooed over his with 'Out '86.'"

"Not good enough?" Gorky said.

"Billy knew what he was doing. He was telling Butch to go fuck himself. So Butch and Chucky decided to teach Billy a lesson and also send a message to anybody who thought they could fuck with them.

"Butch engineered the whole thing. He and Chucky brought in Johnny LaSalle to help with the job, so it was the three of them."

"Plus you..."

"Like I said, I was only the driver."

"Go on," Marko said.

"They didn't plan on the kids being home, because originally they were gonna get to Billy's house during the day. But Butch kept waiting for the gun to be delivered to the Guerneville meet, and it got later and later. Then, when it finally got there, Butch took time scraping off the serial number."

Gorky asked, "Who delivered the gun?"

"It was LaSalle," Mapes said.

"Butch told me to drive Chucky Verdugo's green Chevy van to Billy's house in Fort Bragg, and when we got there, Butch said to park on the grass behind the house. Butch had the gun, and he went in first. Chucky had a knife, and he and Johnny LaSalle followed Butch inside.

"Next thing happens, I hear a woman screaming. Then two gunshots. The woman's still screaming. There was another shot, and the screaming stopped."

Mapes said he needed a cigarette. Gorky handed him one from his pack of Marlboros and lit it. They watched Mapes inhale, taking a break.

"I went to the screen door at the back of the house," Mapes went on. "Billy was sitting there, tied to a chair, crying in pain. Chucky had used the knife to cut off the tattoo. Then I heard Butch yell, 'Get her!' and I saw Verdugo running toward the front of the house. Then Butch jammed the gun in Billy's mouth and pulled the trigger."

Marko said, "You saw Butch shoot Billy in the head?"

"Yessir, I did."

"And you would be willing to tell this story under oath?"

"Yessir, if you would be willing to help me out."

Marko regarded Mapes, a guy who'd obviously played the game of police tag before. "Don't worry about that right now," Marko said. "We'll work things out. What happened next?"

"After Butch shot Billy, he ran to the front of the house, screaming, 'Kill her! Kill her!' but I guess Verdugo couldn't do it. Butch took the knife from Verdugo and slit the little girl's throat. He handed the knife back to Verdugo, and they ran out of the house.

"When we got back to the van, Butch grabbed the can of

kerosene and went back inside. He came back out, still holding the can. Then he jumped into the front seat, and we took off. I looked in the rearview mirror, saw the house burst into flames.

"Butch was out of breath, shouting at Chucky about not being able to kill the kid. I remember him saying, 'It don't make you less of a man if you kill a little girl!'"

I must've looked at him the wrong way, or something, 'cause he said the same thing to me—'You heard me, didn't you, asshole? I *said*, it don't make you less of a man to kill a little girl!'"

Mapes was quiet after that, like he'd said what he needed to say.

Then Gorky asked, "What happened to the gun?"

"Butch threw the casings out the van window somewhere along the road, I don't remember where. Later, when we crossed a bridge over a creek or maybe a small river, Butch told me to stop. He got out and threw the gun into the water."

"And the gasoline can?" Marko asked.

"It wasn't gas, it was kerosene," Mapes said. "I think they left it in the van."

Marko knew that the gun would be key circumstantial evidence. He wanted it. He said to Mapes, "You are going to take us back to that bridge and we are going to find that gun. If we don't, all bets are off."

Mapes said he thought he could find the spot.

Marko wondered about that. Possession and distribution of fourteen keys? At this point, Mapes would probably rat out his own mother to save his ass.

NORTHERN CALIFORNIA

41

EVEN THOUGH THEY all knew it was a long shot, Marko, Gorky, and DEA Agent Raymond Jarvis went through the federal red tape to transport Mapes back to California to help find the gun.

Mapes was booked by the DEA on federal drug charges, so technically he was in the custody of the U.S. Marshals Service. For Mapes to assist in a California murder investigation, the District Attorney of Mendocino County would have to file a writ of habeus corpus to the U.S. Marshals and to the Assistant U.S. Attorney in Detroit.

Gorky called his Mendocino County prosecuting attorney, who knew all about the case, and dictated the narrative for the writ over the phone. As soon as the writ was granted, Marko and Gorky took official custody of Charles Harvey Mapes. That meant handcuffing Mapes there in his cell, heading for the airport with Agent Jarvis at the wheel, then filling out more paperwork for the airline.

At the airport gate when boarding time came around, Marko, Gorky, and the handcuffed Mapes boarded first, trying to be as low-key as possible, hoping not to distress the other passengers. Mapes was handcuffed in the back and wore a jacket covering the cuffs, but it was pretty obvious what was happening, and everybody seemed to know.

They put Mapes in the window seat. Gorky and Marko traded off sitting next to him so that he was handcuffed to one or the other for the entire flight. When he went to the restroom, both Marko and Gorky went with him, uncuffed him so he could pee, then recuffed him again. Being careful, Marko making it very clear to Mapes that if he tried to run they would kill him.

Marko knew how it went.

A guy in your custody is your responsibility. You can't let your guard down for a second. A guy in your custody fleeing with your handcuffs is dangerous to the public. This is bad. A guy getting away while wearing your handcuffs is embarrassing—something your agent-friends will never let you forget. Marko knew this because a handcuffed hooker once ran from one of his Metro copper partners in Vegas. The guy was heaped with scorn and derision and had to pay for drinks for years to come.

Marko knew he had to be on his toes for this one.

———————

BACK IN THE Bay Area, Marko, Gorky, and Mapes routed the trip from Guerneville to Fort Bragg and back. Then they took a ride to help jog Mapes's memory. They did it first during the day; then they did it at night. Then they did it again during the day. When Mapes wasn't with them, he was in a holding cell in Santa Rosa.

The bridge on which Charlie Mapes finally settled was along California Highway 128, somewhere in the Anderson

Valley between Philo and Boonville. Wine country. It wasn't the first or even the second or third place they stopped, but Mapes finally recognized the spot where he pulled the green van to the side of the road so that Butch could hurl the gun into the water below. This time he was positive. This was the place.

Now it was up to Marko, Gorky, and the other law-enforcement personnel who had arrived to help with the search. The first thing they did was reenact the scene by throwing a red-painted .357 handgun from the bridge in order to establish a general location and perimeter for the search. Then divers were sent down into the river. The river wasn't particularly wide, but it was quite deep in places and filled with rocks, boulders, and brush. They looked everywhere. The search continued for two days but with no luck locating the firearm. Mapes continued to insist that this was the place. It was in there, somewhere.

Finally, on the morning of the third day, when they focused near the bank in the mud, one of the divers called out that his instrument had hit on something. They dug around in the mud until the brown handle of a handgun appeared. When they washed it off in river water, they could see the .357 stamped on the Smith &Wesson barrel, but not the serial number. It had been scraped off.

They shouted up to the others, "We got it!"

Marko and Gorky slapped each other on the back. Mapes, handcuffed to the bridge railing, did a little one-armed dance. He knew—they all knew—that the find substantiated his credibility. Who but someone at the original scene could have led them to a .357 buried in mud?

Now that they had it, what were the odds that it was still

operable? Or that the barrel would still produce striations to match the bullet they had in evidence. Or (and this was a real long shot) that the serial number could be raised and traced.

———————

TREASURE ISLAND, named for Robert Louis Stevenson's novel, was created in 1937 from fill dredged from San Francisco Bay. It sits just off Yerba Buena Island in the Bay between Oakland and the city. It's where the ATF forensic lab is located, and where Marko brought the recovered .357 handgun and the spent bullet taken from the murder scene. This particular ballistics job went to Clive Barnum, a firearms expert at the lab and a friend of Marko's.

Barnum would have to clean the gun and test-fire the weapon in the lab's water tank. Then he'd attempt to match the striations, lands, and grooves from the test-fired bullet to the one that was recovered from the Derhammer murder scene.

Marko told Clive that he would gladly assist, and Barnum handed him the .357.

When Marko fired the gun, it still functioned as designed.

"Holy shit," Marko said. "How lucky can we get?"

Barnum took the test-fired projectile that Marko had shot from the .357 revolver and placed it onto the lab's high-powered microscope, next to the spent bullet from the murder scene.

For a quarter of an hour, Barnum compared both pieces of evidence side by side. Was this the same gun used at the Derhammer scene? Marko waited, watching the older man stare through the eyepiece.

Finally, Barnum lifted his head and smiled.

"It's a match," Clive said.

Marko let out his breath, slapped Barnum on the back so hard that the older man started to cough.

"What a day," Marko said. "What a beautiful fucking day."

42

MARKO WASN'T THE most seasoned agent in the ATF, but he did know what the journey toward prosecution was like. The most driven, effective, and concerned cops and agents put their hearts into the important cases. Often, every piece of evidence and every witness they're able to get is a struggle. Like hauling a punk like Charles Mapes back from Detroit. Like spending more than two days on that bridge on Highway 128. Like baby-sitting Angel for weeks in Vegas. Agents get emotionally vested in their cases, they secure all the evidence, then, all too often, the U.S. Attorney or DA says they don't have enough to go ahead with a prosecution.

This is exactly what Marko was afraid of. He'd known the disappointment and frustration before, and knew he would blame himself if it happened again. So even though he was excited about Barnum's verdict on the firearm, and even though he was sure that Roy Gorky would feel the same, still, what he was thinking about was that the threshold for prosecution was very, very high.

Marko paged Gorky, hoping the detective would call back

soon so that he could give him Barnum's ballistics news. Gorky had been sitting in a dimly lit bar not all that far from the Derhammer murder scene. Marko got a call back within minutes.

"The slimeball isn't going to be too happy with us," Marko said.

"Have we got him?" Gorky said. "Have we finally got him?"

"Roy, we ain't got nothing yet."

———————

THEY MET THE following morning at the ATF office to write their affidavits to secure arrest warrants for Butch Crowley, Chucky Verdugo, and Johnny LaSalle. The warrants they wanted would be for four counts of murder and conspiracy to commit murder, and arson.

Both of them were concerned that their star witness would have to be Charles Mapes. Yes, he was better than nothing—and without Angel, what they had was nothing—but Mapes was no prize. The punk would help them prove motive, opportunity, and method. He had brought investigators to the murder weapon of at least one of the victims. And it was obvious that only someone who'd been at the scene that night could be so precise with reenactment of the crime and method of operation and transportation.

Also, Mapes's description of the murders paralleled almost exactly what investigators thought might have happened—except that in Mapes's version, it was Butch Crowley who killed all four victims. In addition, the weapon that Mapes led them to in the river was now forensically linked to the crime scene. And the fact that Mapes knew the accelerant used in the arson was kerosene, not gasoline, greatly enhanced his credibility, at least circumstantially.

But—it was a big *but*—to investigators, prosecutors, and a jury, he was still just a streetwise punk charged with possession and distribution of fourteen kilos of cocaine, some guy who was copping a plea. He was spilling his guts to save his ass.

While Marko and Gorky were knee-deep in paperwork, a call came in from Clive Barnum at the Treasure Island lab.

"I've got something more for you," Barnum said to Marko.

Marko motioned to Gorky to pick up an extension.

"I guess your perp didn't know how deeply they stamp serial numbers into weapons."

"Just a dumb punk," Marko said.

"...who did a dumb job," Barnum said. "I used some chemicals on it and raised the number."

"Clive, you're a magician."

When Marko hung up with Barnum, he called the National Crime Information Center to see if the serial number matched anything in their files.

They got back to him while he and Gorky were still at work on the affidavits. According to NCIC, the gun had been stolen in a residential burglary in Vallejo, California, in May of 1985. The police report indicated that, according to the victim, the suspect was an Iron Cobra named Johnny LaSalle.

This would put the murder weapon in LaSalle's hand. And, according to Mapes, it was LaSalle who delivered the weapon to Butch.

Marko almost couldn't believe this latest piece of luck.

The next thing he did was pay a visit to the 1985 burglary

victim, Jerry Chopp, to ask him why he thought LaSalle had committed the burglary. It turned out that LaSalle was known as a thief in the neighborhood, and he'd threatened Mr. Chopp and his wife during a traffic altercation.

Marko thought about his own neighbors in peaceful little Novato. A thief next door, or a chatty older woman? A hard-working plumber, Little League coach? Or a bank robber or pedophile? Who really knew anything about anybody.

Thoughts like this made Marko wonder if he'd become a permanent cynic. How much time did cynics spend actually being happy? Did they live shorter lives than other people? He thought about the cynics he knew and realized that they were all cops.

———

IT WAS QUITTING TIME. He wasn't seeing Marnie tonight and didn't have any other plans. He wished he could sit down at a blackjack table, take his mind off things. Maybe he'd go to Harrington's Pub, a dive bar but convenient, just across the street from 450 Golden Gate Avenue, popular with ATF agents, attorneys, Secret Service agents. He could watch the game, have a beer or two or three before heading for home.

His buddies Larry, Jim, and Tony were sitting at a table in a smoky, dingy corner of the bar, strategically located to have the best view of the action on the big TV. Marko pulled up a chair. He'd been bragging all day about the Bulls phenom from North Carolina, a guy named Michael Jordan who was just in his third year as a pro.

Drinking beer, watching a game, being one of the guys. What could be better? Then, as they all watched, amazed,

Jordan put on a clinic. By the time it was over, MJ lit up the Pistons for 61 points and a 125-120 overtime victory.

Marko couldn't celebrate too late into the evening because he had work to do tomorrow, hoping that an arrest warrant for Butch Crowley would arrive on his desk. He drove home, half in the bag, north over the Golden Gate Bridge.

Could he be optimistic about the Bulls? He thought he could manage it.

43

"I GOT 'EM," Gorky said into the phone. "All three warrants, right here in my hot little hand."

"Let's get on it," Marko said.

They had twenty-four hours to bring in the suspects. After that, the warrant information would be entered into NCIC, and the arrest warrants sealed so that they wouldn't be publicized. Nobody wanted the suspects to start running.

Johnny LaSalle wasn't hard to find. He was locked up in Florida on a weapons charge. He would be extradited to California, visiting the Golden State once again, this time wearing shiny silver bracelets and an orange jumpsuit.

Finding Butch Crowley and Chucky Verdugo was another matter. Marko wanted Butch badly. He didn't want to wait for Butch to be picked up on a routine traffic stop, or for the punk to come across Metro's radar. And he certainly didn't want to wait for Butch to attack or kill again. Thinking of the attack on Marnie ratcheted up Marko's hatred for Butch another notch. Finding the scumbag was his job, and now it was personal.

Marko called Dexter to see if the big biker had heard anything.

"Butch isn't exactly welcome around the clubhouse," Dexter said.

"Persona non grata," Marko commented.

"Huh?"

"You been there lately?" Marko asked.

"Yesterday," Dexter said. "Guy named Drago Neff's the new president."

"Things changing fast in Vallejo?" Marko said.

"Butch always thought Drago was a rival. I guess he was right."

"You know where Butch is?"

"Not for sure," Dexter said.

"Where do you think he is?"

"I heard Chucky's still staying somewhere south of Vegas. Maybe Butch went to see Chucky. Mohave County, Kingman, Bullhead City—lots of bikers around there. Not necessarily Iron Cobras, but other clubs, or unaffiliated. Butch might be Mr. Popularity with them now that the Cobras aren't taking him back. Or maybe he went back to Vegas."

MARKO HAD GOOD reasons to start with Vegas. His law-enforcement connections were there, and Vegas wasn't very far from Laughlin in Nevada and Mohave County in northwestern Arizona.

There was also the chance to look for Angel. Marko thought Angel must be in contact with Loretta, who was staying out in Henderson at Teddy's place. He couldn't imagine that she would return to the Bay Area. If he could find her in Vegas, he'd let her know about the arrest warrants. Tell her that her troubles with Butch would soon be over.

Wishful thinking—for her and for him.

Also, Marko had heard from Vegas Metro that a new confidential informant was working with the Vegas police and the DEA. The informant was deeply enmeshed in the biker gangs and their drug dealing, so he could be the resource that Marko needed.

Good reasons.

And there was something else. Even though Marko knew that he would miss Marnie, and even though he didn't relish the idea of going up against a violent killer, going to Vegas would give him something he'd been missing.

He'd been away from the blackjack tables for a while now. He didn't want to admit it, but it had been getting to him.

How much of his decision was based on that? Duty to the badge, or just more of his dirty little habit?

44

MARNIE STOOD NAKED at the big sink in her bathroom. On the counter were bottles and jars of expensive lotions and creams. The drawers were filled with cosmetics, brushes, every type of implement for applying makeup, all of it courtesy of her job. Most women would love to have all that expensive stuff, hundreds of dollars' worth—powders, pencils, lipsticks, beautiful colors that could transform one's looks—for Marnie, however, it was mostly about business. Over the sink was a big well-lighted mirror, but she didn't especially want to look at herself. On her right cheek, alongside her nose, was an abrasion that was healing but still quite red. Her doctor had told her that the redness would fade with time. In the meantime, she would use one of the expert concealers sitting on the bathroom counter. Except for the red area, it seemed like her face and body were almost back to normal. Did that mean that her life was getting back to normal, too?

For maybe the twentieth time, she wondered if she had any role in the attack. Had she been careful enough? Was there something she shouldn't have been doing? Was it her fault, even in some small way, that Butch had been able to get to her?

Marnie knew very well that Marko blamed himself for what had happened. Maybe she blamed him too, but she hoped not. In the hospital, he was at her bedside for practically the whole two days—missing work, probably bored to death, enduring the hospital atmosphere and routine. Even though she was so numbed from painkillers that she could hardly speak, she told him he wasn't responsible for something that another person does. Especially when that person is a sociopath.

Then Edward had come to visit and stayed for hours. So difficult for Marko and Edward to be thrown together like that—and her, looking and feeling worse than she ever had in her life, barely able to talk. But there was nothing to be done.

Butch. What a monster. She hadn't been able to see his face clearly that day. He'd pulled a stocking down over his head, and the way it distorted his features, she was sure it was more frightening than actually seeing his face would have been. But she had seen the black goatee. Too bad it wasn't possible to prosecute with just that. Oh, well. They'd get Butch someday, and there was a much greater price waiting for him to pay.

Marnie went back to the bedroom, opened her big walk-in closet. Since the attack, she'd had to limit what she wore. It hurt to pull things over her head, belts and jewelry were out, and high heels made her feel unstable. She settled for a loose shirt that buttoned down the front and a pair of sweat pants. Not her usual style.

Two days ago, Marko told her that he'd gotten the warrant for Butch and he was going to Vegas to track him down. That was it, that was the decision he'd made.

The idea terrified her.

She had tried to get used to all the special-agent stuff (it was, after all, Marko's life)—the fact that they couldn't always reach each other, the secrecy, the potential for violence. She knew all about it.

And this vicious, brutal man Butch, who didn't seem to have normal fears or hesitation... She was taking all of it much more personally now, which made her understand how close to the whole Derhammer thing Marko must feel.

Last night he had come over after work. He'd grilled a chicken for her, baked a couple of potatoes, made a nice salad, and they drank a bottle of wine. He had been so sweet, so thoughtful. It really touched her. She told him she wished he wasn't going away.

After dinner, she drew a bubble bath for the two of them in her big tub. She wanted him, wanted to make love with him, but her ribs were still so painful, it made her afraid to be touched. It seemed like he understood. But their last night together.

He said he'd be away only a few days, maybe a week, but Marnie thought it would be longer.

And what if something happened? That was the thing.

LAS VEGAS

45

MARKO HAD FLOWN into Vegas last night, picked up a rental car at McCarran, and headed straight to Sam's Town to play some blackjack. Now he was back in his hotel room, away from the Strip. An old movie, *Laura*, was playing on the TV, the sound muted. The female lead—he thought it was Gene Tierney—reminded him of Marnie. The old guy in the movie, a skinny character called Lydecker (Marko knew it was Clifton Webb—the one and only), who's obsessed by Laura, is about to kill her, but instead he's shot by the young, good-looking cop. Marko was pretty sure it was Dana Andrews. Andrews had those hard eyes, perfect for the cop role.

Marko unmuted the sound just as Lydecker uttered his final words: "Goodbye, Laura. Goodbye, my love." A nut case, but a terrific movie.

Sometimes Marko felt obsessed too, but when it was about Marnie it felt good. Like feeling her breasts against his side when they were lying together in bed, his arm around her. Her head would rest against him and he could smell her hair. It was chestnut-colored, and shiny, like the flanks of a thoroughbred.

He liked that comparison but thought Marnie wouldn't.

He would run his hand down her side, settling into the valley of her waist, letting it rest; then he'd stroke her back. Her body would move into him, her thigh pressed against him. An invitation.

The night before last, in the San Rafael condo, Marnie had said that he was starting to look like a drinker, telling him he was too young to have red cheeks and bags under his eyes. She'd said it lovingly, but there it was.

Marnie drank, sure, especially when they were together, but he knew that she watched herself around liquor. Even when they were having fun with it, which was almost always. Maybe he had bags under his eyes, but he thought she needed to loosen up a little.

He'd had more than a few beers today, wanting to take one with him in the car when he headed back to Sam's Town. First he'd drive around, maybe past the old MGM Grand, which they were now calling Bally's. If he got stopped by the cops it was no problem. He still knew everybody in Metro.

Marko's thoughts wandered back to a day six years ago, when he was a rookie street cop in Vegas. He had just changed into plain clothes after a ten-hour shift when the call came into Metro South that the MGM Grand was in flames. He knew it was bad because sirens began to shrill all over town and dark-gray smoke was billowing over the Strip and Flamingo Road.

Two hours into the blaze, the death toll was twenty-seven and counting. By early afternoon, word was spreading that they might run out of body bags. More than fifty dead by then, the bodies taken to a nearby grade school, a temporary morgue.

Marko had been ordered to get some sleep, then report

back to work the fire on a double shift. When he was back in and suited up, a chopper carried him to the MGM roof, dimly lit by generated light, and when they landed, someone handed him an ax. He could see body bags lined up, loaded into the chopper as soon as his squad got out. With the ax in one hand, a flashlight in the other, and a gurney on each shoulder, he began the hard walk down the stairwell.

At Floor 19, he heard a fireman yell, "We need seven over here!"

Seven what?

Corpses lying in the pitch-black hallway, needing to be tagged and bagged. All these from smoke inhalation. The flames hadn't made it up this far. He and his partner bagged them, carried them up to the roof. Over and over again.

Marko and the others all worked on pure adrenaline, in a nightmare of shock and disbelief. The blaze in the casino downstairs had been a fireball, so fast and intense that it took players with cards still in their hands. Hours later, Marko waded through six inches of water to a charred craps table— the very one where he'd tried to learn the game just a year before. He picked up a pair of melted, soot-covered dice, put them in his pocket.

More than six years now since the MGM Grand went down, but that didn't matter. It was with him every day.

————————

HE DECIDED TO close his eyes for ten minutes before heading out again, not wanting to miss more time at the tables, but the Fort Bragg fire, and the little girl Dallas, appeared as soon as he drifted off. Maybe what he needed instead was a cold drink. A glass of water this time, with lots of ice.

He got up, opened the sliding door to the balcony, let the desert air rush in. It felt soft, like Marnie's skin. There were lights on in the pool three floors below, a young couple fooling around in the shallow end, bobbing and floating together in the bright water.

He went to the bedside table, picked up the phone, and dialed her number.

"Hey, babe," he said when she answered.

"Marko. How are you, sweetheart?"

Her voice enfolded him. He could feel his breathing slow.

"I went out for steaks with a couple of the guys." Lying. Stupid. He'd known her for months now, and she still thought blackjack was something he did for fun.

"You just home?" he asked.

They talked about little stuff.

"I miss you, Marko," she said finally, pulling him in.

"I miss you too," he said. He knew he didn't want to lose this one.

They said good-bye, and he put down the phone. He picked up his keys and wallet, put on his jacket, and headed for the door.

His hand went up to the baggy place beneath his eyes. Wet. He must be crying.

46

MARKO WAS BACK in the city of odds—every move he made confirmed it. What were the chances of winning five hands straight? The probability of being dealt a natural blackjack? Or the odds that the Bulls would win tonight?

But it wasn't just the gambling. Gambling generated the atmosphere, but then it seeped into every corner of life. Like when he thought about Angel. What were his chances of finding her, hiding out in some corner of Vegas? Or the odds that, if he went to a certain raunchy biker bar, he'd get some snitch to rat out Butch, or even that he would run into Mr. Scumbag himself?

In Vegas everything was a bet, and usually he liked it that way. It made things more interesting. But when it came to finding Butch Crowley, taking chances was something he wanted to avoid.

Marko wondered if Butch knew that for twenty-four hours in California there'd been a warrant out for his arrest, that his wanted status was now national, entered into the NCIC. The certainty of it was comforting.

He thought of Butch's surly face appearing from beneath the pickup truck that day last October at Angel's. Marko had seen a lot of bad faces during his time in law enforcement: losers with nothing, blank-eyed criminals in stir, the permanently drunk, the terminally addicted, the withered faces and broken teeth of meth freaks, desperate people who needed money or drugs or alcohol more than anything in the world; Butch's face, with its arrogant smirk.

Was it really possible that Marko had actually seen Butch only that one time, other than in a mug shot? He had imagined Butch's face so often—full of rage when he killed the Derhammers, when he shot Gordo. Now, especially, the face obscenely covered by a stretch of pantyhose when he attacked Marnie, the black goatee flattened against the chin like the wing of a black witch moth. Sometimes he couldn't get it out of his mind.

He had the sudden realization that the case had become an obsession. Amazing. Had it really taken him so long to understand this basic fact of his life? What if he hadn't met Marnie, who helped him get a perspective on all of it? Of course, Marnie herself had become an obsession, but a good one, one that he didn't mind. Or was her hold over him simply the power of pleasure?

THAT NIGHT MARKO played blackjack and finished in the money, bigtime. He played for four hours straight and won a little over four thousand dollars. He had a few drinks along the way, and when he got back to the hotel, he was exhausted. He barely got out of his clothes, barely managed to take a leak before crashing on the bed.

He'd been smart enough to let the impending exhaustion lead him away from the casino. Even with the winning streak, if he played for twenty minutes longer he would lose his concentration and most likely his money. It was one of his rules: never play when you're tired.

Back when he was a cop with Metro, Marko didn't make much money. In 1980, the night he graduated from the police academy, he'd gotten drunk and very stupid. That night he lost his entire paycheck on blackjack at the MGM Grand, and it was a big lesson for him.

From that time on, Marko would take fifty dollars a week and go to Sam's Town every Friday after work to play. If he won two hundred dollars he would walk away; and if he lost the fifty, he would walk away. Things were easier when there were rules, especially when you were young.

But winning or losing, money didn't mean that much to him, not then, and not now. Marko just wanted to be comfortable. Easy come, easy go. He figured his attitude was the result of spending time at the tables and the sports books. No better place to see the way the world worked; that, and listening to his dad, who knew about life.

When Marko was a kid, once in a while his dad would tell stories about his own Depression-era childhood. His mother— Marko's grandmother—would steal coal off boxcars to keep the family warm in winter. It was Chicago, with the wind and the snow.

These days, Marko hated the cold. San Francisco was just right; Vegas, when it wasn't summer, was even better. He knew he needed to take a step back, walk around in shirt sleeves, enjoy the warm dry air.

Like his dad used to say, it was all relative.

47

THE NEXT MORNING, Marko went down to the hotel pool for a swim. He cruised the bottom of the pool, testing how long he could stay under, feeling like a fish, all alone in the blue water, the bright sunlight making everything sparkle. Back in the room a half hour later, he called Loretta at Teddy's Henderson Compound, and they set a time to meet. When he was dry and dressed he headed over to Sam's Town for a couple of hours, first stopping in at the casino restaurant for the huge buffet breakfast that they offered daily. Marko was hungry. While the slots jangled in the background, he ate scrambled eggs with cheese, bacon, sausage, and a couple of big pancakes. Until the meeting time he played some blackjack, figuring as usual that mornings at the casino would keep him from drinking while he was playing.

When it was time to head out, Marko retrieved the rental car and drove to Henderson. Good thing he'd called ahead to Teddy's place. There was no way he would have gotten inside otherwise. A big goon was waiting for him as he pulled up to the gate, the kind of gorilla you want on your side in a fight.

Marko maneuvered the car into a paved area down below the big house, walked up a curving flagstone path lined with a dozen different types of palm trees. He went up to the front door and rang the bell.

Loretta opened the thick wooden door. Teddy's initials, elaborately carved into the wood, surrounded the peephole like a family crest. She led him through the front hallway, where an oil portrait of Teddy, ornately framed in gilt, hung in solitary splendor on lemon-colored walls.

In the big front room, she said, "You want something to drink?"

"It would be nice to have a coke or something," Marko said.

Loretta went to get the soda, and Marko looked around. It had been quite a while since he'd been here. The first and only time was when he was a new Metro copper, and Teddy had some business he needed official help with.

Everything about the house was bigger than life. The living-room walls were lime-green. A heavy ceramic ashtray took up half the coffee table. The base of the low glass table was made from a huge old tree root or a driftwood log or something. Marko couldn't really see it with all the stuff piled on top—a big bowl of nuts, another of candy, a thick photo book of nude women. The rug was such a deep shag it made him want to take off his shoes. Like being at the beach.

Loretta came back, handed him the soda, and sat on a long orange couch. Marko sank down into the overstuffed cushions of an armchair, next to a big tank of tropical fish. Out through the tall glass wall, where the backyard stretched into the surrounding desert, Marko could see Teddy's sixty-foot pool, a waterfall flowing into it, an oversized hot tub off the deck.

"So, how're you doing?"

"Getting better."

Loretta looked pretty good for having survived a gunshot wound to the head. Not like before, but pretty good. She'd been so lively that day he met her at the bar with Angel. Animated. Loretta, he thought, didn't yet have any real energy. She was healing.

"How's it going, living here?"

"I'm staying in the guesthouse out back with another girl. It's nice. Teddy leaves us alone."

"So, you heard from Angel?"

"I don't know where she is," Loretta said.

"Where'd she tell you she was going?"

"They told me at the hospital that Angel came to visit. That was the last time I saw her, but I was still unconscious, so I guess I didn't really see her. If she told me anything, it's buried so far down I can't get to it."

Loretta was sounding smart, Marko thought. Had the gunshot somehow activated a heretofore untapped area of her brain? But then, he hadn't really known her before the attack. He did know that you could never tell with sex workers. You might assume they were dumb, but you'd probably be wrong.

Maybe the enforced rest had given her time to read some Freud, an activity Marko was saving for his old age. When he was a movie critic.

"Has she contacted you since?"

"Not a word."

Even if Loretta had heard from Angel, would she tell him? Marko knew he didn't really understand women, but he felt that the answer to that one was no.

"Lemme know if you hear from her," Marko said. "We could take her into protective custody, keep her safe from Butch."

Loretta just looked at him. She wasn't going for that one.

———————

AFTER HE LEFT LORETTA, Marko drove back to Vegas and over to Teddy's Bar—see if anybody there knew anything about Angel. The place wasn't very populated, so Marko had his choice of bar stools. A girl he'd once dated was sitting at one of the tables with a couple of guys. She and Marko went out together for maybe a week and a half, which had been a long-term relationship for him at the time. From where he was sitting, she looked great, cute and sexy—a pouty mouth, tight blouse, showing off her tits. Marko got the bartender's attention, ordered a beer. The girl—he remembered just in time that her name was Judy—walked over and leaned against the stool next to his.

"Hey, Marko. Where you been?" She gave him a big smile, flashed her blue eyes at him. Her lips, he noticed, were hot pink. Marko looked down at the hand she put on his arm, saw that her fingernails were the same color. Electric pink. The color buzzed.

"Hey, beautiful," he said, swiveling on the stool to face her. He started flirting, putting on the moves, feeling like the old Marko in Vegas.

But then Marnie came into his head, almost like she was sitting next to him.

This was definitely something different.

Suddenly, Judy didn't seem so available. Was it just Judy, or was it other women too? He looked around the bar, but there weren't any other women around just then.

Did loyalty to Marnie count when the two of them weren't even in the same state? When he wasn't even sure what they'd promised each other?

He guessed it did.

Oh, well.

———

THAT EVENING, Marko went over to Fabian's house for supper. Ralphie had set the table outside on the terrace overlooking the pool, in the cool early-evening desert air. Juana fixed a dish made with shrimp and sausage.

"It's called paella," Fabian said. He opened a bottle of wine, poured generously. When they finished that bottle, he opened another. Marko knew it was the good stuff—Fabian always drank the good stuff—but to him it was a matter of indifference, or maybe mild curiosity. It wasn't Marko's thing, except for once in a while with Marnie. If Marko wanted to buy a nice bottle of wine to bring to Marnie's, he just went by price.

Fabian, Marko thought, had his life set up. So did Teddy. Fabian lived mainly in his head. Teddy lived in his head too, but even in late middle age, Teddy's brain was still in his dick.

Marko wondered where his own brain would be when he was fifty.

———

ASLEEP IN HIS hotel room that night, Marko was visited by nightmares. Tonight's feature presentation involved muzzle flash, but unfortunately it wasn't from Marko's gun. In his dream he was reliving a night when he could easily have died, but the perp was a bad shot and missed Marko three times. Marko revisited that event on a regular basis, popping up from sleep.

There were other close-call dreams. Like the time he'd arrested a guy but missed finding a small Derringer hidden behind his arrestee's belt buckle. The only reason Marko didn't get shot was because he had shown the guy some respect. He barely escaped that one.

And the night Marko hit a kid with his police car while driving to a hot call on the Vegas Strip. The kid's face smashed against the front window right in front of him. That one frequently woke Marko up in a cold sweat.

Then there was the helplessness dream. As a patrol officer Marko once pulled a dead Asian girl out of her backyard swimming pool. Marko never witnessed a family go so crazy. They were in such a frenzy that they would not let the coroner take the body of the twenty-year-old, who had left behind a suicide note. "No, no, no..." They said it over and over. He didn't even know if they spoke English. The girl was distraught because her boyfriend broke up with her, so she drowned herself. What a horrible waste.

From time to time he considered seeing a shrink, but he knew he wasn't neurotic. It was normal to be upset about stuff like this. These days they were calling it PTSD. His dad, the World War II vet, would have called it shell shock or maybe battle fatigue.

Marko looked at the clock after the muzzle flashes forced him awake. It was the middle of the night. He knew he wouldn't be able to go back to sleep, at least not right away. The longer he stayed awake, the less chance the dreams would come back.

He could go to a casino. Even at three in the morning, there'd be people playing.

Instead, he picked up the remote from the bedside table and turned on the television. It was Ray Milland in *Lost Weekend*—the movie where the hidden whiskey bottle hangs outside the window. Milland, the master of sophisticated desperation, had won an Oscar for this one. It was right up there on Marko's list of the top-ten most depressing movies ever made. Tough, very tough. Yeah, okay, it turned out all right in the end, but getting there... He thought of Roy Gorky, and of the phone conversation he'd had with Gorky's wife. Would Gorky come through this and still have his family?

After ten minutes Marko turned off the set, deciding he'd try to go back to sleep. Too much alcohol, that's why he'd seen the muzzle flash. Too much drinking always brought on the nightmares. He used his best trick—replaying a game in his head, trying to remember every play. Baseball, football, hockey—it didn't matter. It was a jock's version of counting sheep.

48

IN THE TWO and a half days since Marko had gotten to Vegas, he'd taken the rental car and repeatedly cruised by every biker-related bar, tattoo parlor, and hangout he knew of in town and in North Vegas. He spent an hour in the dark, dirty Paradise Strip Club on Industrial Road, chatting up some of the lower forms of life that were drinking at the bar, knowing that his quest for information in such a place was futile. From there he went to the Diesel Dugout on East Sahara for some watery beer, the music blasting so loud it made Marko's head ache. Then on to Hog Haven on Boulder Highway, just south of Sam's Town, where the beer was cheap and very cold. The owner was a thick-waisted, rough-looking woman named Carrie, who rode a Harley. Her sleeveless shirt showed off the spider-web tattoos running down both her arms.

Next came Snake Eyes Tattoos, located on Las Vegas Boulevard just north of Sahara since the mid-1970s. It specialized in biker logos in colorful ink. Cash only. The back room, Marko had heard, was for poker and dice games and the occasional sex party.

The only biker clubhouse Marko knew of in the area was a concrete-block establishment in North Vegas. The building itself looked like a combination bunker and gone-to-hell frat house. It was surrounded by a chain-link fence topped with barbed-wire, with a large padlock on the entry gate. Motorcycle parts and engines were scattered around the yard. A funky carport on the side of the house shaded the bikes. Empty beer cans, a barbeque pit, and some shitty lawn furniture completed the picture. No sign of Butch or his bike.

Marko knew he was grasping at straws, treading water, buying a single ticket for a million-dollar lottery. Whatever inroads he was making into the Vegas biker scene were leading nowhere. The confidential informant who was in with the bikers and knew about the drug deals, the one who was working with the DEA and Metro, would have to come in sooner or later. Marko's Metro buddy, Detective Mike Raleigh, said that the CI was due to report in the next day or so. That would be Marko's chance.

In the meantime, Marko decided just to wait. That was okay. Usually he hated to wait, hated surveillance most of all, which was nothing but waiting. But in Vegas, at least he knew how to pass the time.

One time when Marko was young he'd gotten beat up really bad. It was 1971, high school, and he'd gone out with his buddy Louie, who had a very fast blue Buick. "Louie Buick" was what all the guys called him. While they were stopped at a traffic light, another fast car, a Chevy Super Sport with tinted windows, pulled up next to them. They could hear the engine rev, inviting them to drag race down Cicero Avenue. Then the Super Sport driver rolled down his window and spit on the

Buick. That's when Marko got a good look at him.

Marko turned to Louie and said, "That jagoff just spit on the Buick!"

"That little cocksucker," Louie blurted back.

The light turned green and both cars peeled out. The Super Sport had the lead for the first quarter mile, but then Louie turned it on, passed them, and cut them off. They were pissed.

Marko and Louis, thinking they'd lost them, pulled into an Arby's at 78th and South Cicero to grab a celebratory bite to eat.

No sooner did Marko open his passenger-side door then the Super Sport pulled in next to him. All four doors opened, and six guys got out. Three went for Marko and three went for Louie, and the fight was on.

Marko got in a few good shots at the beginning but he was badly outnumbered, hit so hard he saw shooting stars. Finally, when it was over and the beatings stopped, the Super Sport punks loaded back up and sped away. Marko and Louie lay there on the pavement next to the Buick. Sirens were shrilling in the distance, so they hurried as best they could to get back in the car and leave.

Louie dropped Marko off at his parents' house, where he quietly slid in through the back door, just wanting to get to his bed and not be seen by his parents. He lay there in pain— broken jaw, broken nose, and blood all over his face.

Then his dad turned on the light. "Jesus Christ," he blurted out. "C'mon, we're going to the hospital."

Marko, who had been in a few scrapes before, convinced his dad he would be all right. Before his father turned out the light he asked Marko if he got in a few good shots of his own.

Marko said, "Yeah, on all three of 'em."

Marko's dad said, "Atta boy," as he flipped the light switch.

A MONTH OR SO LATER, when Marko was mostly healed, he and his brother Cliff were at Gas City at 55th and Pulaski, filling the tank of their dad's car. As luck would have it, a blue Super Sport pulled in at the next pump. As the driver got out and went to put gas in his car, Marko smiled to himself. It was the same punk who'd spit on the Buick.

When the punk went back to sit next to his date in the Super Sport's front seat while the tank was filling, Marko walked over and gestured for him to roll down his window. The kid, seeing his face, looked panicky and wouldn't do it, so Marko grabbed his jacket and wrapped it around his right hand. With one pissed-off swing, Marko smashed out the window, grabbed the kid, and pulled him out through the broken window. He beat the shit out of the guy as the girlfriend sat there screaming.

Marko and his brother got back into their dad's car and drove away. Good old Chicago street justice at its best. Yes, he got his chance at a little payback, but in the long, slow month before that, all he could do was wait it out. He had to wait for the broken jaw and the broken nose to heal.

Now, Marko had just spent much of the past month watching Marnie get over her injuries. He'd seen the bruises fade, the pain subside, health gradually take over. Her job had been to put everything else aside and get better. Mostly it was a matter of waiting.

He wondered about his waiting time here in Vegas. When it was over and he knew where he was going, how would things turn out? He couldn't picture it. He remembered the wish he'd had a few months ago, to heal the picture of the little girl, the place where her neck had once been whole.

Whatever happened, he needed to be ready.

49

BUTCH ROLLED A FAT J, using some of the good stuff he'd brought with him from Vallejo. He knew that by now he must be a wanted man, and that sooner or later they would be coming to get him, even here in piss-poor Bullhead City.

How did he even get here? His good buddy Chucky, who was probably as wanted as he was, had led him to this paradise—Laughlin's dirty little backyard. Chucky and his fat Bullhead biker mama Marlene, a real ton of fun. Chucky, who couldn't keep himself from going after anything that moved.

Butch might like the place a whole lot better if he didn't have to look over his shoulder every minute, which was not a good situation for a man who wanted to ride free. His plan, as far as he had one, was to use Bullhead to get himself together, then move south to Mexico. Plans could be good; they had their place. He just needed to think some more about this current one.

When he was in school, a report he stole from the school counselor's desk read: "hyperactive, easily bored, lacks self-discipline." Then, that same week, one of his teachers had told him to his face that he was impulsive. Impulsive? What did that mean? That when something happened he responded? That he didn't just wait around before he took action? Wasn't that why he'd been chapter president in Vallejo—because he knew what he wanted to do and he did it? Like going after Novak's girlfriend, even if it brought down more heat on him... even if now that seemed like another mistake?

If he had to lay low, Bullhead didn't seem like such a bad place to do it. There were business opportunities, a lot of like-minded people, proximity to foreign places—a land of opportunity for someone like himself. Butch chuckled as he took in a big drag of reefer, contemplated the quality of the weed. Fuck, he sounded like he was looking for a job in a bank.

The problem with Arizona, as he saw it, was that there was no fucking water. You could ride forever and not see anything that wasn't all dried up. At least Bullhead City—the locals called it "BC"—was near the Colorado River. But that didn't really qualify as water. It was more like a great big ditch. Tamed by Hoover Dam way before he was even born.

When Butch thought of Mexico, on the other hand, he thought of the beach. Maybe that was wrong, not how it really was, but he liked the idea. Thatched tiki huts near the surf, fishing nets, hot sand but okay because just a few feet away you went swimming. Everybody tan. Were there bikers at the beach? Had he ever been to the beach, sat in the sand drinking a brew?

His original idea when he got here was to hook up with some of the meth cooks in the Bullhead area. Every other guy around here cooked crank. And everybody around here used something—all the time. This was the druggiest place he'd ever been, and he had to admit it wasn't pretty. Be good instead to get a distribution thing going down in Phoenix, where there was plenty of demand. But that brought in the exposure factor, and right now he needed to be invisible. In Bullhead he wasn't alone in that situation. It seemed like half the dudes around here were on the lam.

His new line of work was going to be guns. Running guns to Mexico. Mexico already had enough drugs. He'd have to be cool about the gun business, or connected, because the Mexican gun laws were tough. Especially after Arizona's open-carry laws. In gun-crazy Arizona you could wear your piece to the supermarket or the liquor store. Not that the laws applied to him, a convicted felon, who couldn't carry a gun to the toilet. Not that he was alone in that regard. As far as Butch could tell, there were more felons in possession of a firearm in dusty little Bullhead City than in the entire Bay Area.

In Mexico, on the other hand, the laws against guns were so strict that when you brought one across the border to sell, the markup was maybe three hundred to five hundred percent. Buy a gun in BC for two hundred bucks, sell it in Mexico for eight hundred, or even a grand. At least that's what he was hearing. It was the scarcity factor. Butch might not have much cash right now, but he had access to a bigger arsenal than he'd ever seen before. These Bullhead City gun dudes were something else.

When he got to Mexico, he didn't particularly want to stay in Gringo-ville, so he would have to learn some Spanish, more than the ten words he already knew, like Donde esta el dinero? Maybe Mexico wasn't such a brilliant idea. He'd have to ask around. Were there guys like him there? What the fuck, man.

Where were there guys like him? He'd never met one.

Butch went to the tiny wreck of a bathroom to take a piss, looked in the scarred mirror. Shit. He loved his pointed goatee, his long black hair. The Sultan of Harley.

But the time had come to change the way he looked.

50

ON THE THIRD day of his enforced R and R, Marko got a call at eight in the morning from Mike Raleigh. Mike relayed the address of a nondescript building on Industrial Road, said that if Marko got there by ten o'clock, room number 122, he'd be able to meet the confidential informant.

The wait was finally over.

When Marko arrived at five minutes to ten, Mike, a DEA agent named Roland Cooper, and the informant were sitting around a metal desk in the first-floor room, drinking coffee from cardboard cups. The space, with its empty, pale green walls was so bland, so anonymous, it looked like a meeting room at a mid-priced chain motel, rented by the hour.

Mike was wearing a white shirt and khaki pants; Agent Cooper wore a suit and tie. The informant had on motorcycle boots, a black sleeveless T-shirt, and baggy camo pants held up by a thick leather belt from which dangled a heavy chain and a big set of keys.

He was a deeply tanned Anglo, with relaxed gestures, who went by the name of Curly. His actual name was Carl Renfro.

His scruffy blonde hair was long and braided, and a few loose strands coiled into ringlets at the back of his neck. His hair was so sun-bleached that it looked almost white. In another, much younger, tamer life, he might have been a surfer.

It was almost unheard of for law enforcement to land an informant inside the outlaw-motorcycle-gang structure. They were lucky with Curly, at least that was how it was going so far. This is what Mike had told Marko, so Marko knew that he had to respect the relationship and go slow with what he needed from the informant.

Mike had said that Curly decided to inform on the outlaw motorcycle gangs after witnessing a particularly horrific crime perpetrated by the brothers in his chapter. It involved gang rape, torture, and subsequent murder.

Not exactly business as usual, but given the range of criminal activity that Marko understood to be part of the outlaw-biker criminal repertoire, not surprising, either.

Curly wanted money for his information, and he wanted immunity in exchange for his work. The feds, Marko knew, hadn't made him any specific promises, but they knew that the payoff from Curly's work in the drug underground would potentially be huge, and they were being careful to cultivate the relationship.

Marko studied the CI. The guy smelled vaguely of motor oil and cigarettes. His muscular arms were covered in tattoos. His fingernails, which he was cleaning with a pick, were embedded with grease. There was a band of twisted leather on his left wrist, and the four rings that he wore carried the usual biker insignias. Everything about his appearance said outlaw.

Marko had brought two mug shots with him—one was a

shot of Butch Crowley, the other was of Chucky Verdugo.

"These are the guys we're looking for," Marko said, laying the mug shots on the desk. "Have you seen either of them?"

Curly studied them, the DEA man looking over his shoulder.

"This one, no," Curly said, pointing a finger at Butch. "This one, maybe." He picked up the Verdugo photo.

"Maybe?" Marko said.

"He looks like a guy I saw in a bar in Bullhead City. A place called Mad Dog's Cocktails. It's a bar and strip club."

"What else?"

"I think he's a full-patch Iron Cobra, but not from Arizona. He hasn't been around long."

"Anything else?"

"There's gonna be a biker rally in Laughlin this weekend. A word-of-mouth thing. Maybe your guys'll show."

"And if they do?" Marko asked.

"Maybe I can give you a call, for a small fee."

"That would be awful nice. You know the G has a lot of cash."

Curly just smiled as Marko gave him his pager number.

So that was it. Marko tried not to feel disappointed. What had he been expecting? In spite of Curly's protestations about the crimes of his buddies, the guy was a snitch-for-hire. He was another Charlie Mapes.

If Marko hadn't decided to wait around for the informant, he could have left for Laughlin and Mohave County two days ago. At least Curly had given him the possible lead for Chucky Verdugo in Bullhead City. Dexter had also mentioned Mohave County and the Bullhead area. It might seem like the end of the earth once you got there, but it wasn't far from Vegas.

Vegas Metro was the law-enforcement entity for unincorporated Laughlin, Nevada, just across the Colorado River from Bullhead City. When the meeting ended, Marko talked with Mike out in the hallway.

"You'd be a lot more welcome in Mohave County than me."

"No shit, Sherlock," Mike said.

"So how 'bout taking a little ride with me?"

"I could probably manage that," Mike said.

"Got any nice unmarked rides?"

"Now, that's gonna cost you."

"What else is new?"

Laughlin wasn't very far. They could get there in a couple of hours.

51

BUTCH STOOD IN front of the mirror in the trailer's tiny bathroom, turning his head from side to side to take in his new look. He was holding a pair of scissors in his right hand, a comb in his left. Yesterday he'd walked the half mile over to the Carefree Trailer Park, where Chucky was living with Marlene, his Bullhead old lady. Marlene leased a double-wide at the park, with a screened-in porch, a carport, and a storage shed. It was nice, comfortable, had a big window on one side. It was only ten feet from the next trailer, but private, like a real house— bougainvillea growing up the side, oleanders in the little yard.

During the day, Marlene worked at Ardelle's Beauty Shop in Golden Valley and usually got home late in the afternoon. Butch showed up at her place just after five, waited in the yard for twenty minutes until she arrived, then asked her to cut his hair. When it wasn't pulled back into a ponytail, his hair hung down almost to his shoulders, black and straight. Except for the stint in prison fourteen years ago, he'd worn it long since he was a teenager, since right after he was kicked out of school. Even though he wasn't young anymore, had turned thirty-seven last month, his hair was still full. It was his little vanity. His long black hair and his goatee.

Marlene sat him in a tall chair, covered his shoulders with a towel, and went to work with the scissors. She cut it short all over, leaving it longer at the neck. It felt strange, and Butch didn't want to see what she'd done. He waited until he got back to his trailer to look in the mirror.

When he finally did take a look at himself, it took him the whole night to get past the change. It didn't look bad, nothing like the prison shearing, but it wasn't how he wanted to look. It wasn't him. It felt like he had submitted to something, like those times when he was a kid and his father locked him in a closet. He had a momentary flash of anger at Marlene but decided that was stupid. He'd asked her to do it.

Now he had to take off the goatee. His trademark. That was something he needed to do it himself, control the process. Would he shave? No, he'd leave a week's worth of beard. Better to keep the cover.

Holding the scissors in front of his face, he parted the blades. It felt like he was about to cut off part of his body, but in one swift cutting motion he took off the whole goatee. There it was, a handful of five-inch black whiskers. It was over. Now he looked like someone else.

First there had been his Iron Cobras colors: Before he left the Bay Area for Arizona, Butch had packed away the leather vest with the rockers, the patches, the things he'd worked for. He'd ridden over to Bullhead wearing his plain black-leather jacket. Now the hair, his wonderful hair, and the goatee. What would be next? It made him decide that when he finally got to Mexico with some money in his pocket, he was never going to come back. This was going to be the last compromise.

For the rest of his life he would look however the fuck he pleased.

52

LATE SATURDAY AFTERNOON, the days were getting longer and warmer. In his real life back in Vallejo, Butch would be at the clubhouse, downing some brews, ready for an all-night party. His real life? So much had happened since the Derhammer thing that his so-called real life was moving farther and farther into the distance. Mexico, his new life, was calling.

Yesterday, Chucky told Butch that he was going across the river to Laughlin for a bike rally. It wasn't the big annual Laughlin run, where bikers came from all over. This one would be some local bikers from Nevada and Arizona, and some from California who couldn't wait for the River Run next month. Sort of a practice party on two wheels. The Golden Nugget and Riverside parking lots would be filled with the roar of custom choppers, a warm-up for the big event.

Chucky had heard a rumor that some Mongols might show up. Iron Cobras rivals from L.A. If the Mongols were there, that could mean anything. Butch loved a fight, loved getting it on, and he could hardly stand the thought of not heading over there, but he'd warned Chucky about putting himself in a situation where there were lots of cops, undercover and otherwise. He told Chucky that getting arrested would be a bad idea, but Chucky said he didn't think the pigs would be a problem.

Butch told himself that he was being smart, staying in the shadows until he got his business situation together. He was doing what had to be done. But it felt like he hadn't been out since forever—caged up in this shitty little trailer, where now he couldn't even stand to look in the bathroom mirror.

Finally Butch couldn't take it any longer. He thought, okay, it's gonna be dark soon, take the bike out for a little ride in the desert. Feel free for an hour. He hadn't seen a cop in days. If there were any in the area, they'd all be across the river in Laughlin.

Butch's bike was stored in an old wooden outbuilding next to the trailer. It was a stand-out bike, one that would be noticed. He put on his jacket, went out to the shed and unlocked the padlock. The chopper was facing out, the way he always left it. He ran a rag over the bike, mounted up, fired up the thousand-pound machine. Beautiful. With the engine rumbling beneath him, suddenly everything was okay.

He pulled out of the yard onto the street, past the scrubby, fenced-off land in this part of town, headed over to 95, which was the long strip of paved road that made up Bullhead's main drag. He rode past the park by the river where the lowlifes slept, past the RV sales, the Dream Girls' Gentlemen's Club, the Sit-n-Bull barber shop, the tackle shops, the thrift stores, the adult bookstore, the Bullhead Superlube, the three or four slot-machine repair shops that serviced Laughlin's only industry, past the cotton fields on the south end of town, turning east on

Boundary Cone Road. Boundary Cone ran up from the river, up past the batch plant, toward the hills and mountains in the distance. Butch liked how the scene changed—the flat desert plain near the river—once a wide floodplain when the Colorado ran free—and then into the hills, some of them rising straight up, twelve-hundred feet from the valley floor. Up top, Boundary Cone connected with Old Highway 66. Butch felt like he was in the Wild West when he rode the winding, fifteen-mile-an-hour curves of 66, up through Sitgreaves Pass, then down toward Kingman.

IT WAS AFTER dark when Butch pulled the chopper up to the wooden shed in his yard and killed the engine. He felt like a new man after the ride, nearly forgot about his shorn head. He could hear the phone ringing inside the trailer, but by the time he pushed down the kickstand, got to the flimsy front door, and jammed the key into the lock, the ringing had stopped.

He went back out, backed the bike into the shed, ran a rag over her flanks, locked his baby inside.

53

WITH MIKE RALEIGH behind the wheel of the big unmarked Ford, and Marko in the passenger seat, the two men rode south on Highway 95 from Las Vegas toward Laughlin. When they got to the Laughlin Highway they turned east, then crossed the big river into Arizona where the road became 95 again, the main drag through the long narrow town of Bullhead City along the east side of the Colorado.

In among Bullhead's seedy retail buildings, they looked for Mad Dog's establishment, spotted it on the south side of town between the Sit-n-Bull barber shop and a convenience store. There were a couple of bikes outside the bar, neither of them belonging to Verdugo or Crowley. Inside, the place was almost dead. A women who looked to be around forty, with a good body but a hard face, was dancing topless for the half-dozen male customers. It was Saturday, and Marko and Mike figured that the regular patrons were probably at the bike rally. They headed back across the river to Laughlin.

The rally wasn't hard to spot. Maybe two hundred riders and their choppers hanging out in the parking lot of the

Riverside Resort. The Riverside was Laughlin's first hotel and casino, the place that started the 24-hour-a-day action in this smaller, cheaper, quieter casino strip, a family-friendly cousin of Las Vegas. In the daytime, the unincorporated town was a tacky strip of high-rise buildings scarring the magnificent landscape; at night, great swaths of neon glitzed everything up, making it seem like a glamorous gambling oasis in the middle of nowhere. Bullhead City, its immediate neighbor across the wide Colorado, had become a low-rent suburb for hotel and casino workers. The grittier reality of Bullhead was an ugly, crime-ridden little town, with more than its share of meth cooks and tweakers, dealers in illegal guns, chop shops, a long list of sex offenders, and punks like Chucky Verdugo and Butch Crowley.

Marko knew that he would find them there.

———————

TWENTY MINUTES INTO their bike-rally reconnaissance, Marko spotted Verdugo in the middle of an altercation between two rival gangs. In his mug shot, Verdugo's broad forehead and prominent features made him look like a much bigger man, but he was medium-height and wiry-looking, almost skinny. The bikers were shouting each other down, posturing with their chains and ballpeen hammers and whatever else they carried as part of their gear.

"They're all drunk," Mike said. The parking lot was littered with cans, bottles, cigarette butts, fast-food wrappers, and here and there a torn piece of clothing. It looked like hell to Marko, but the bikers seemed to be having a good old time.

Verdugo looked over at Marko and Mike—strangers in street clothes who stood out like altar boys in a whore house and were moving around to where he was standing—and his expression changed.

"He's seen us," Mike said.

"And he's gonna run in about two seconds."

Marko and Mike were muscling their way through the crowd when Verdugo took off. Marko was still pretty fast from his athlete days; the skinny punk Verdugo was probably shit-faced, but he darted easily through parked bikes and around cars, finally coming to an open area of the huge parking lot where he could run. About fifty yards out, shouting for him to stop, shouting that they were police, gaining on him, Marko tackled him. The guy fell hard.

Mike sat on Verdugo's back while Marko, winded, cuffed him.

"Chucky, Chucky, Chucky..." Marko said, getting his breath back and fastening the bracelets. "I'm afraid the party is finally over."

VERDUGO, IN CUSTODY at Laughlin Metro on Civic Way, seemed surprised by the NCIC warrant but obviously knew what the deal was. Brought in on a capital murder case, and California carried the death penalty.

"Okay, asshole," Marko said during the interrogation. "Let me tell you a little secret. We got Charlie Mapes on fourteen keys and, guess what? He's singing like a fuckin' bird. We know you didn't kill anybody; we know it was that piece of shit Butch. But you can help yourself out here if you tell us where to find him."

It took a while, but finally they got Verdugo to drop the

dime on where his good buddy Butch was staying. When he gave them the street name and described Butch's trailer, Marko couldn't believe his luck.

54

LATE SUNDAY MORNING, Butch woke up to the sound of the telephone. It had to be Chucky, calling to tell him what went down last night at the rally. Nobody but Chucky had this number; nobody else would be calling him anyway. He glanced over at the clock. It was late, but still too early for Chucky to be calling, especially if he had any kind of a time last night.

"Yeah," Butch said into the phone.

"Hey, Butch, it's Marlene."

"Marlene, baby. What's happening?"

"Chucky didn't come home last night."

"Oh yeah?" Butch stopped himself from saying anything else while he considered the situation. The first thing that came to mind was Chucky alone at a biker rally. He picks up some nice-looking little bitch, a girl weighing maybe a hundred pounds less than Marlene. They get a room, stay over in Laughlin. Chucky being Chucky. That was how Chucky had met Marlene, after all. Had she forgotten?

The next thought was of the cops. Chucky arrested.

"I was thinking, the rally's still on," Marlene said. "Maybe you'd go over there, look around for him?" Marlene said.

Butch thought, no way. If Chucky couldn't take care of himself, Butch wasn't going to do it for him.

"I'll see what I can do," Butch said before hanging up, telling her he'd let her know when he heard something.

If Chucky was just having a good time, then fine. But if the cops had picked him up and Chucky was in a tight spot, would he rat out Butch? The biker code, did it still apply? They were a long way from Vallejo, and Butch wasn't trusting anybody these days. Besides, he'd warned Chucky not to go over there.

Butch thought things over for a few minutes. This was not part of the plan. He didn't want to leave today. He wanted to get back in bed and sleep for another five hours. He was sick of doing things he didn't want to do.

He lay there for ten minutes, thinking about what might happen if he didn't make himself get up, get his stuff together, and get out of there.

What stuff? He was in this Bullhead shithole; he'd ridden over here on his bike. Except for what was in his saddlebags, he'd left everything behind. He'd left his colors, his club, being the president—now even his hair. He'd left his life behind. Yeah, well, that meant another kind of freedom, didn't it? He could go anywhere.

Arizona was a big empty place, and on the other side of it, not all that far, was Mexico. It would be easy to leave Bullhead, head straight to the border. The border was full of holes that he could ride through. People were saying it wasn't always going to be that way, that someday there would be a big wall keeping people out; keeping them in, too. But not yet. He had no money to speak of, but maybe he could hook up with some Mexican bikers, get some action going when he finally got down there.

Butch had slept in his clothes. He reached for his .45. Then he dug out the little handgun and his knife. What else was there? At the last minute, he grabbed the weed he'd brought with him, stuffed it into a bag. If they stopped him, a half kilo of marijuana wasn't going to make any difference. Shrugging on his leather jacket, he went outside, not bothering to lock up behind him. He headed to the wooden shed for his bike.

55

SUNDAY MORNING, Marko and Mike had been sitting in the big Ford sedan for almost two hours. Marko flashed back to the day last October, watching the Vallejo house where Angel lived with Butch. It seemed like years ago. And how far had they come with the case since then? Not very. It was amazing how frustrating and time-consuming his job could be. Months of effort, and now maybe, maybe, they were on Butch's doorstep.

The two of them had spent a long night at Laughlin Metro. Verdugo fell down pretty hard when Marko tackled him, and he was drunk, so it was a while before he said something coherent. He hadn't given up anything about the Derhammer murders, but finally, almost sober and understanding the position he was in, that's when he had given up Butch.

Nothing here yet on this gritty little street. The trailer they were watching looked like any other, and there was no sign of life inside. What did Marko expect? Maybe Verdugo hadn't given up Butch after all.

They couldn't go up to the door. If there was some chance, some little chance in hell, that they'd spot Butch, then they would call for backup. Laughlin Metro knew where they were, and they'd also alerted Mohave County law enforcement, covering both directions of escape, Nevada and Arizona.

FROM WHERE THEY were parked, down the block and on the other side of the trailer from the wooden shed, they didn't see the man right away. Marko raised the big binoculars. Was it Butch? He wasn't sure. Short hair, no goatee. But then the man turned his way, and he saw the expression. No mistaking it.

"It's him," Marko said. "I'm positive."

A minute later Butch was on his chopper, turning onto the street. He pulled out past them, roaring off. Mike started the Ford's engine, made a U-turn, and spun out behind. When Crowley took a north-south side street, then turned up Silver Creek Road toward the mountains, Marko radioed the Mohave County Sheriff. They were staying in Arizona, at least for now. Mike turned on the flashers, and Butch sped up quickly, his chopper's big engine rumbling and roaring up the hill.

Silver Creek Road led east, away from the river, a good straight road for maybe a mile. Butch was hammering down on the chopper's throttle, but for the moment they were still with him.

Before very long they were well outside the town, with the vast, empty valley spreading out on both sides. The wide, straight road quickly gained in elevation—and that's when it changed. Suddenly it turned from pavement to gravel, then, not much farther on, to dirt, narrowing to a one-lane road.

Then came the curves.

The big Ford spewed rocks and threatened to spin out on

almost every turn. The bike raced ahead. Butch must have known who was behind him before he turned up Silver Creek. It was the perfect road for a bike. Marko, belted in, holding onto the passenger strap above the door, sliding on the seat as the car slid, had to admit that the way the chopper took this road was a thing of beauty. Mike swore each time he spun out around a curve. His knuckles were white from holding the wheel.

Then Butch was out of sight. They kept on, still fast, but they were losing ground, losing Crowley. The terrain was brutal for a big sedan, and the suspension on this automobile had seen better days. There were rocks in the roadway, and Marko hoped that the tires were in good shape. They wouldn't be worth shit after this run.

The dust in front of them from the chopper's wake settled then disappeared. Had Butch turned off a side road? A path up ahead, or maybe one that they had already passed? One where they wouldn't be able to follow? All they could do was keep following, watch for the bike, and hope that the Mohave County Sheriff would be able to cut Butch off at the other end.

56

THE LAST TIME Butch looked down at the chopper's gas gauge, it was hovering on empty. That was miles back, he'd been riding full out, and now the engine started to sputter.

This was it. He had to come up with something, now. He spotted an old dirt road ahead on the right. It looked rough enough that maybe the big sedan wouldn't be able to follow. He turned the bike sharply, the powerful brakes almost taking the wheels out from under the machine. Skidding, throwing up gravel, he made it onto the side road, righted the bike, and gunned the throttle. But after twenty yards, the roadbed turned into dry wash. Bouncing over rocks and fallen branches, barely under control, he rode over the rutted wash as far as he could take the bike. Finally it stalled out.

Butch hammered his fist on the handlebars in frustration.

He banged down the kickstand, threw his leg over the bike, dismounted, looked around, and started moving toward the cliffs. He scrambled up a rise, toward a falling-down old tin shed, a place that would give him cover. As he ran, he turned to look back, drawing the .45 from inside his jacket, scanning the hillside below. And that's when it happened.

It was like a leap into space. Suddenly there was no more ground beneath him. No footing beneath, no place to stand. He was falling, falling. Where was he... where was the ground? He managed to grab hold of some rock, enough to right himself, but then he was sliding and tumbling, down and down and down, bumping against the slick side of the shaft as he fell, the length of his back scraping along something protruding out into the hole.

FOR A WHILE there was nothing. When Butch came to, he was half sitting, half lying, stunned. He was at the bottom of a hole. It was so deep that daylight barely reached him. He didn't know how far he had fallen. Everything around him was dim, and everything was cold.

He was sprawled in maybe six inches of water, and below that was muck, which felt like it was sucking at him, pulling him down. He didn't seem to be able to move his legs. His leather jacket was bunched up in the back near his shoulders, and it felt like there was a rip down the length of his spine.

He didn't feel any pain at first; but after a while it started up. A few minutes later it was more than he could stand. When he tried to move, it was excruciating. He bit the sleeve of his jacket, so hard his jaws hurt, which worked for a moment, but then his body screamed again. He moaned, rocked back and forth a little, but the movement hurt too much. He leaned his head back, looked up to the top of the pit. A hole of light far above him. It made him dizzy.

Time hovered and passed. Everything suspended.

It seemed like forever.

The next time he forced himself to look up, he saw a spot of light moving toward him. The beam of a powerful light was curling around down the hole. Eventually it found him at the bottom.

Somebody shouted down.

"Crowley... you alive?"

Butch could hardly speak. He squinted, looked up to the top of the pit, saw the outline of a head.

"...yeah..."

"Crowley, can you hear me?"

Butch realized that he'd mumbled the word. He raised his head, which had fallen on his chest, tried to shout.

"YEAH..."

It was so painful. He felt himself drifting in and out of consciousness. What came into his head was a memory, the terrible beating from his father. Painful, but nothing like this. He thought of the time he dumped his bike, broke his shoulder. Another time, a fight he'd been in, he and his buddies against a rival club.

It was a while before he heard the people up above shout down at him again. Then someone yelled, "Listen up, Crowley. We're going to get you out of there. But first you have to give up your weapons."

Silence.

"We're going to lower a bucket. Put your weapons in it. Then we'll work on getting you out."

Butch watched as the rope snaked slowly down the side of the pit. When the bucket got near him, he could hardly raise his hand to it. But there was something hopeful in seeing it there, attached to the outside. He knew he wanted to be outside.

He shifted slightly, painfully, and managed to reach the little handgun in his boot. He still had the .45, held onto it even falling down the shaft, like it was glued to him. He would send up the little gun, and maybe the knife too, a switchblade, if he could get to it. Keep the .45. Maybe there would be some chance at the top. Get them before they got him. Take them all out.

He stopped planning, stopped thinking. At least he was still breathing.

He waited for his ride.

57

BY THE TIME the Sheriff's Department volunteer search-and-rescue unit had rigged the scaffolding—a triangle of aluminum beams rising six feet over the shaft—the working lines, the five pulleys, and were ready, first, to bring up Butch's weapons and, then, Butch himself to the top of the abandoned mine shaft, there were fourteen people on the scene: three deputies from the Mohave County Sheriff's Department who were also technical-rope specialists; seven search-and-rescue volunteers from the rope team; EMT personnel from the Western Medical Center in Bullhead; and Marko and Mike.

Marko watched as the bucket supposedly carrying Butch's weapons reached the top of the shaft. One of the sheriff's deputies picked it up and brought it over to him. Inside, Marko found a small-caliber handgun and a switchblade. Was this the entire weapons stash that Butch took with him to the bottom of the pit? He doubted it. But there was no way to know and no way to take this any further now. They would have to deal with it as Butch was being pulled out. The job now was to get Butch out of the shaft and take him into custody.

The mine shaft was an ugly place for an accident. Local law enforcement told Marko that the area was peppered with them, that there were thousands of open shafts in Arizona alone. So many shafts, too few resources to find them, fill them, fence them. If a shaft was on private land, it was up to the owner to assume responsibility and liability. Some of the shafts had been hand dug as early as the 1880s during Gold Rush times. This particular one was blasted out, a later excavation. Its hard-rock walls were slick, except for some mining timbers and pipes protruding from the sides. Marko wondered how many animals had fallen into such pits. Were there carcasses at the bottom with Butch?

The shaft must have been at least sixty feet deep. Hauling out a man wouldn't be easy. He wondered about the extent of Butch's injuries, about the toll it would take on him, being hauled up. Not that Marko cared much for Butch's well-being, but he speculated about the confrontation when they finally got him out.

Normally in a mine-shaft accident, they'd send down a search-and-rescue worker who was a technical rope specialist. He'd rappel down the shaft, stabilize the victim, secure him in a sling that would be hauled to the top. But because Butch was dangerous and probably still had weapons, they decided to send down a victim-harness. If he could get into it by himself, fine. If not, they'd send down a rope tied with a buntline hitch—over, under, around, and through—which wouldn't slip. Butch could slip it over his head, fit it around his back and chest, under his armpits. They'd haul him up with that. Painful but expedient.

If Butch couldn't manage that much, well, too bad. A well-deserved end. Marko knew it wouldn't come to that, but it would certainly be an easy end to the case.

———————

WHEN BUTCH WAS about fifteen feet below the surface, Marko and two of the deputies drew their guns and waited. A foot at a time, Butch rose up the shaft, the working line straining on the pulleys, the harness biting.

Marko shouted down to him. "Crowley, we are waiting for you with guns drawn. Try something and we'll kill you."

Silence.

"Crowley—do you understand?"

No answer.

"If I see a weapon, I will shoot you before you reach the top. Got it, Crowley?"

Still no answer. Marko wanted to cut the line with the switchblade and send the punk back down the shaft.

Then Butch's head finally broke the surface of the shaft, and Marko understood the situation.

Butch was unconscious, his arms hanging limp at his sides.

After all this, it was the easiest arrest Marko had ever made.

NORTHERN CALIFORNIA, SEVEN MONTHS LATER

58

THE CALIFORNIA NEWS media was buzzing. The prime defendant in the most heinous murder case in Mendocino County history was about to come to trial. Gerald "Butch" Crowley would be brought before the bar of justice on capital murder charges.

Marko, sitting in his office, looked at the calendar on his desk. It was four days until showtime at the courtroom, and he knew they would be getting things together up in Ukiah, already impaneling their jury.

The ordeal last March at the abandoned mine-shaft was played out many months ago, but that surreal day in the mountains above Bullhead City, hauling Crowley out of a sixty-foot hole in the ground, was with Marko like it was yesterday.

So much had been at stake—a killer on the loose, the high-speed chase, the adrenaline, the uncertainty. A chase like that, and then the waiting—waiting for the Mohave County patrol officers to get there and then for the search-and-rescue team to arrive, all the methodical preparation at the top of the shaft, forcing Butch to surrender his weapons, the rescue people carrying out their courageous work, watching them haul the rope through the pulley system, up, up, up, a foot at a time, one foot up for every five they pulled. Then, finally, what did they have? An unconscious man.

It would have been fine with Marko if that was the end of it, but no such luck. Instead, it was just another turn of the wheel of justice. Butch Crowley wasn't going to be shipped straight from Bullhead to death row. Criminals came up against the justice system. And so did law enforcement—from the other side. Marko granted that the system was a good thing, but he also knew that he didn't want this scumbag walking the streets, ever. What were the odds that Crowley might be free in a couple of weeks? Unfortunately, they were pretty good.

If, through some combination of hard work and good fortune, the prosecution got a conviction and Butch faced the death penalty, what would that mean? Maybe twenty, twenty-five years on death row? Butch might be with us until 2012. By that time, where would everyone be? By that time, the whole world could change.

At the top of the mine shaft that day, Marko had fantasized about getting a water truck, filling up the whole shaft, but the scum would probably have floated to the top. He also thought about just shooting the bastard—pulling the five-shot from his ankle holster, walking to the edge of the hole, and firing away.

Unbecoming thoughts. He had a lot of them.

From the time that long day had finally ended, from then on it had been paperwork, suit-and-tie stuff, the pomp and circumstance of court appearances, and now, maybe, a lot of disappointment. Monday he would be sitting in a Ukiah courtroom, determined to help prosecute Butch Crowley. He was sure he'd remember not to get his hopes up.

LATE THAT AFTERNOON, Marko gave Marnie a call at work.

"Hey, babe, how you doing?"

"Good, but I'm so busy," Marnie said. "We just got three new people to train."

"You wanna take in a movie later? *The Untouchables* finally made it to Novato."

"I can't tonight, Marko. I've got a meeting in an hour with some company people from New York."

"Maybe I'll catch it anyway."

When Marko was a kid, the television series had been a staple of his early TV viewing. The whole family sitting around, watching Eliot Ness and his team of handpicked agents—the courageous and uncorruptible Untouchables ("they couldn't be bought off—they were untouchable")—go up against Al Capone's criminal empire during the 1930s. Robert Stack played Ness, and Walter Winchell narrated. Marko could still hear Winchell's odd, clackety-clack voice. The series ran from 1959 to 1963. Marko was a boy, and it was fifty minutes of heaven.

Tonight, Marko went alone to the seven o'clock show. Sitting in Novato's newest movie theater, a tub of buttered popcorn in his lap, Marko had to admit that, at least in the movie version, Sean Connery stole the show. At one point, Connery, playing the Irish beat cop Jimmy Malone, as incorruptible as Eliot Ness himself, tells Ness to be ruthless: "He pulls a knife, you pull a gun. He sends one of yours to the hospital, you send one of his to the morgue. That's the Chicago way, and that's how you get Capone."

That's the Chicago way! Marko wanted to pump his fist at the screen. That's what he would remember ten years from now when he thought of this movie. Not Kevin Costner's pretty-boy face, not DeNiro's sneering Capone. Even though the Jimmy Malone character didn't make it to the end of the movie, went down in a hail of tommy-gun fire, that's what he would remember from *The Untouchables*.

It was Hollywood's version of Chicago, but Marko could relate.

59

EACH MORNING, Angel read about the upcoming trial in the papers. They gave it more coverage every day. And whenever she turned on the TV, there it was again. Changing channels or watching a soap didn't help. It was her life they were talking about, and there was no getting away from it. They had charged Butch with the Derhammer murders and he was in custody, behind bars and denied bail. Butch Crowley was officially out of circulation.

It had been over a year since Angel escaped from the house in Vallejo, taken the bus to Vegas, then, after the time at Fabian's place, fled to Reno. Even after all these months, she was amazed at the relief she felt now, knowing that Butch couldn't come after her.

The fact that he was locked away changed everything, at least for the time being. But his actually going down for the Derhammer killings? She wasn't going to count on it. She was surprised that it had even gone this far. Butch had gotten away with every other vicious, criminal thing he'd done. Why should this time be different? But hearing about the Derhammer murders now on TV, what Butch had done to that family, it was even worse than she imagined.

She wished she could be brave enough to turn herself over to the cops, walk into the courtroom, and tell everything she knew. She was trying to get up the nerve, but it wasn't easy.

What would she get from testifying? That was the question.

For one thing, she could dump her guilt about staying silent. She'd been carrying it around for the past year.

But if she testified and Butch still walked away from this, she'd have to watch her back for the rest of her life, put her whole life in danger.

Marko and the rest of those cops didn't understand that there was no way they could protect her.

Besides, why would a jury believe what she said? She was Butch's old girlfriend. His lawyer could slam her in court. There was plenty he could say against her. Not about now, so much, because things had changed, but about how her life used to be.

And what if she testified and it didn't go well? Wouldn't that make things worse? The only real proof she had was the photo she'd taken that night when he got back from Fort Bragg. She'd written the date on the back of the photo, but she could have done that anytime. She hadn't actually seen *anything*.

No, it was easier to stay out of it.

Easier, yes, but it felt like giving Butch a huge break. Like helping him get away with this. It also felt like a big step back into the gang life. How many of the Iron Cobras, their girlfriends, anybody else who knew anything about it—people she used to know personally—how many of them weren't talking? All of them. Staying silent out of fear. Maybe they were calling it biker loyalty, but she knew it was fear. She knew what they were like. She didn't want to be one of them, and she didn't want to be afraid anymore.

She had taken all this time off from her waitressing job in Reno, rode the bus over here, not knowing if she'd still have a job when she got back. She was staying with a girl she knew in Richmond, trying to decide what to do.

Twice she had picked up the phone to call Marko. This time when she dialed Marko's office number, he answered.

"Marko, it's Angel."

"Angel! Where are you?"

"I'm in Richmond."

"Richmond? Richmond, California?"

"Yeah."

"Give me your address. I'll come pick you up."

"I don't think so."

"Why not?"

"Because I'm still figuring things out."

"Angel, you gotta testify."

"I'm deciding..."

"You gotta do this."

"Listen, Marko. If I do, it's gonna be on my own terms."

"Angel..."

"I mean it. I know you can get a subpoena, or take me into custody, or whatever the cops do. But if you do, I won't give you what you want."

Deciding to shut up, Marko held his breath, thinking of what to say next. "Okay. Whatever you need."

"I'll call you back," Angel said, and hung up the phone.

All this time away from her job, all this worry and trouble. If she testified, how much longer would she have to be away—

two weeks, three? She needed the Reno job, was lucky to have gotten it.

If she did go through with this, there would be a price to pay.

There always was.

60

MARKO SAT THERE drumming his fingers on the desk. He was so anxious he didn't know what to do next. He didn't want to get up, even to get coffee. He needed to sit there until she called back, not use the phone in case it rang, not leave his desk in case she changed her mind.

Larry walked over, handed Marko a cup of coffee.

"What's up?"

"Believe it or not, I'm waiting for Angel to call me back," Marko said.

"*Our* Angel? She called...?"

"She's here. In Richmond. *Our* Richmond. She's been hearing about the trial on TV."

"You going to bring her in?"

"I don't know where she is exactly."

"So you're going to do what?"

"I'm gonna use the power of persuasion," Marko said with more confidence than he felt. Not that persuasion had ever worked with Angel.

He drank some of the coffee, straightened the papers on

his desk, put his pens and pencils in the pen cup. Finally, he looked up at Larry and rolled his eyes.

When the phone rang again, Marko restrained himself from answering it mid-ring. He didn't have a plan yet. He didn't even have a bluff yet.

"Okay," Angel said. "I've decided I'm gonna testify. Tell me when to be there."

Marko said, "Don't you want a ride up there?"

"Just tell me when to show up."

"You know where to go?"

"Yes."

"You want me to arrange for a hotel room?"

"No."

"Then be there Monday morning," Marko said.

Angel didn't say anything.

"I'll tell them you're coming," he added.

More silence.

Marko finally said, "Listen, Angel, you're doing the right thing."

He heard Angel hang up. Marko put the phone back down, sighed. He thought of the morning Fabian called to say that Angel had slipped out of his grasp, remembered the sinking feeling it gave him. And then, a couple of hours later, hearing from Larry about the attack on Marnie. Both in the same morning. That was an unbelievable day. Most days just slip by and don't matter. That day, he could remember everything he said, everything he felt.

Larry, still leaning against the door frame, said, "You getting a subpoena?"

"Yeah, and where do you suggest we find her, Mr. Ladies' Man?" Marco said.

"Good point," Larry said, grinning at Mr. Tough Guy.

———————

THREE DAYS TO GO. Except for going over every shred of the paperwork, reviewing every note he'd taken on the case over the past year, being available at the prosecutor's table, and testifying at the trial, his part of it was over.

He thought he'd done everything he could. Hadn't he?

Marko considered what the prosecution had going for it. On the evidence side of things, it was pretty weak. They had four bodies but only one complete projectile. The other bullets were either mangled or fragmented or nonexistent. And they had been able to determine that the accelerant used to burn the farmhouse was kerosene. That was it.

As to motive, they had the wire recording of Dexter in the Cobras clubhouse with Butch, Butch blurting out about Billy Derhammer, "That thieving snitch, he got what he deserved." It was a statement that tended to prove motive, but how much was it worth in the courtroom?

Means? In a creek in northern California they found the gun that fired the projectile recovered from the crime scene. Clive Barnum at the ATF lab raised the gun's serial number, and they eventually determined that it had been stolen in a residential burglary from a Jerome Chopp in Vallejo in 1985. According to Mr. Chopp, the burglary suspect was Johnny LaSalle, who was known as a thief in the neighborhood. Johnny LaSalle, an Iron Cobra and associate of Butch Crowley, was now awaiting trial in California for the Derhammer killings.

Witnesses? Charles Mapes was their star witness. His testimony was absolutely vital, and Marko sincerely hoped it would also be compelling.

Mapes had given them the location of the weapon and the fact that Butch killed all four victims. And he'd identified the accelerant as kerosene. These were things that only someone who had been there would know.

But Mapes was a co-conspirator who was plea-bargaining his way out of possession of fourteen keys of cocaine and maybe twenty years in prison. Why would the jury believe him?

After all this, what did they really have? Circumstantial evidence and the testimony of a co-conspirator.

Marko was worried.

Now would they have Angel? And if they did, what would she tell them when she got on the stand?

61

ON MONDAY, Marko pulled out of Novato early and made his way up to Ukiah, the Mendocino County seat, for the opening day of the trial. He was wearing his special suit for the occasion, the jacket on a hanger in the back seat. He'd bought it on one of his shopping trips with Marnie, when she decided to make a respectable man out of him, at least in terms of his appearance. The price tag was maybe four or five times what he thought anyone should pay for a single garment, but Marnie never paid retail, so the suit came with deep discounts. Besides, he liked the way it looked, and it made him feel lucky. He was also wearing the silk tie she had given him, which so far he'd managed not to stain.

At the courthouse, he looked for his seat in the already crowded courtroom, found it directly behind the prosecuting attorney and next to Roy Gorky. Being a case agent meant that Marko was allowed to sit with the prosecution and assist whenever possible, along with the lead homicide detective, so they were ringside for this event.

By the time the proceedings were about to begin, the place was packed. A hush came over the spectators as Butch shuffled into the courtroom and over to the defendant's table. He too wore a suit, quite a change from the orange jumpsuit that was standard issue at the Santa Rosa jail where he'd spent the past seven months at government expense. Both of Butch's legs had been broken in the mine-shaft fall, and he wasn't walking very well. Would this prejudice the jury in his favor? Marko suspected that Butch was too arrogant to play up an infirmity, even though his lawyer probably suggested that he should.

His lawyer, Martin Loftis, was the best defense attorney that dirty drug money could buy. Someone in the Iron Cobras must have coughed up a fortune to get Loftis. Marko speculated that it was more to protect the club's reputation than for any particular allegiance to the former president of the Vallejo chapter. Loftis was a specialist in people like Butch—high-profile cases for scum of the earth who had the money to pay his outrageous fees. In the law-enforcement community, Loftis was thought of as a cold-blooded snake, someone who would do anything to get his clients off. He dressed just like he talked, from his styled hair to the monograms on his crisp white cuffs. Marko knew that Loftis lived in the penthouse of a fancy high rise overlooking Golden Gate Park and the famous bridge, had seen him arrive at other trials in his big black Mercedes, a driver at the wheel. The defense attorney was big on show.

The lead prosecuting attorney for the State of California was James Blacklidge, who was a master at prepping the prosecution. He'd worked tirelessly on the case from the crime scene to the trial, had demanded and got countless hours of work from Marko and Gorky.

The judge, Salvatore Urso, was short, stocky, bespeckled, and no-nonsense—someone who would be in complete control of his courtroom at all times.

Selecting the jury, Marko had heard, had been an arduous process. He looked them over. Eight men and four women, a mix of young and old. All of them were white. The foreman, in his late sixties, wore suspenders to keep his pants up over his paunch. All twelve were perfectly presentable, neatly dressed and clean. One of the jurors bore a strong resemblance to Jack Klugman in *Twelve Angry Men*, a movie Marko had seen more than a dozen years before. He wondered how many of the actors he could still name: Fonda, of course; Klugman, E.G. Marshall, Lee J. Cobb, Ed Begley, Martin Balsam. Who else? Unfortunately, here in Ukiah there wasn't a Henry Fonda in sight.

Marko thought that if he were up against serious charges, he might go for a bench trial, with only a judge to decide his fate. Juries were strange organisms. Unpredictable. How could you trust them to render a verdict solely on the evidence presented? To serve without bias, prejudice, or some vested interest in a case? They were amateurs, after all, with emotions, predispositions, susceptibility to the media.

And what about this idea of a jury of one's peers? Who were one's peers? The old guy with the suspenders? Was he a peer of Butch Crowley?

As for evaluating scientific evidence, like when Clive Barnum testified, how was an amateur supposed to pass judgment on that?

Marko remembered a quote from Clarence Darrow: "Almost every case has been won or lost when the jury is sworn." Or maybe it was from *Inherit the Wind*, Spenser Tracy playing Clarence Darrow.

For the sake of simplicity, he decided to leave intimidation and jury tampering out of this argument he was having with himself. And he didn't even want to think about the idea that not all lawyers were created equal. Not everyone, after all, was Spencer Tracy.

In the end, the matter was really very simple: Butch had to pay. If he didn't, Marko wasn't sure he could live with himself.

62

THE PARADE OF witnesses came and went. For the first four days, Marko sat there listening, taking notes, helping the prosecution with certain points as needed.

Finally, on the fifth day, it was his turn. By the time he was called, many of the expert witnesses and law-enforcement people had already testified: Mendocino and Mohave County Sheriff's personnel, ATF investigators, fire-scene examiners, ballistics experts, the entire team of forensic and medical people assigned to the case.

For one entire morning Marko was on the stand. His direct examination by James Blacklidge lasted three long hours. He first testified about the crime scene and finding the projectile at the top of the stairs; then he responded to Blacklidge's questions about his trip to Detroit months later where he debriefed Charles Mapes; then about Mapes taking them to the spot where they found the gun; about test-firing the gun at the ATF Treasure Island Lab and getting the match results from Clive Barnum. He testified to tracing the gun after Barnum raised the serial number; interviewing Jerome Chopp; then about Chopp naming Butch's friend Johnny LaSalle as the prime suspect in the police report.

It was exhausting. He had testified in many trials, but this one was different. With this one Marko felt the prick of personal involvement—always saying the truth, but at the same time inspecting each word from every angle, weighing its effect on the judge, the jury, the prosecutor, and the cross-examination to come. Mentally, it was grueling, but having that stake in the outcome was what made it exhausting.

When they broke for lunch, Blacklidge came up to him, told him he'd done well. Marko thought he'd done pretty well, too, congratulated himself for being on the right side. He went across the street and down the block to the diner where he'd eaten lunch for the past four days. Giving testimony had made him ravenous. Today, there was barely time for a decent meal to sustain him for Loftis's upcoming attack. On the sidewalk was a blackboard with the day's lunch specials. The meatloaf with garlic mashed potatoes caught his eye. He ordered, wolfed it down as soon as it appeared, then ordered coffee and a piece of apple pie for the caffeine and the sugar.

When the lunch break ended, back in the courtroom Marko resumed his seat on the witness stand, and Loftis went after him in cross. First came the attack on his character—the drinking and the gambling. Marko knew it was coming. He'd been in enough courtrooms, seen it as standard operating procedure enough times: the witness, either subtly or overtly defamed, visibly shriveling as the character assassination progressed. Marko tried to stay cool, hoping the jury would see it for what it was—an opening gambit, just part of the defense attorney's say-anything technique. Not personal, that's what

Marko repeated to himself, even as he wished Loftis a painful death sometime in the near future.

When the defense lawyer finished painting black marks on Marko's character, he went into great detail on one particular point, focusing on the fact that the gun—the alleged murder weapon—was not in Novak's possession from the time it was recovered in the river until it got to the ATF lab.

Even though it took him the better part of an hour, it was a very weak argument because Marko had followed ATF procedures to the letter.

Finally Loftis was finished with him, Marko stepped down, and the court recessed for a short break. It took a while before he stopped feeling the adrenaline that had been coursing through his veins.

Up next would be the state's eyewitness, Charles Mapes. Mapes was their star witness, and Marko, like all of them, needed to be coherent for the rest of the afternoon.

————————

JAMES BLACKLIDGE, in his opening statement to the jury on the first day of the trial, had said that the state's eyewitness would "put each of you at the crime scene that night."

Now, five days later, Mapes didn't disappoint. His testimony was well-prepared and extremely believable. It was also vivid, almost too vivid for some of the jurors. The more he said, the more it became obvious that only someone who had been at the scene would know such precise details of the crime.

Mapes testified to seeing Butch jam the gun in Billy Derhammer's mouth and to watching him pull the trigger. He repeated the chilling words that Butch had yelled in the van that night: "It don't make you less of a man if you kill a little girl." He explained how he was able to take investigators to the exact location of the gun used in the killings. And he asserted that it was Butch Crowley who had killed all four of the victims.

Even though Mapes was bargaining his way out of prison, Marko felt that the totality of the circumstances and the exactness of his testimony were very convincing. And what Mapes said about the recovery of the weapon was too precise for the defense to overcome.

Marko looked over at Martin Loftis and relished the moment.

63

ON THE SEVENTH day of the trial, Marko almost couldn't believe what he was hearing. What name should he give to that welcome sound?

He realized it was the sound of a bombshell, and Angel was the one dropping it.

He hoped the jury was hearing the same sound. He looked over to his right, to the twelve people sitting there. It seemed like they were.

Angel, in a gray cardigan sweater, her face pale, her big eyes wide with the seriousness of what she was doing, looked even more demure, sedate, and anonymous than she had that day at Fabian's, in the kitchen with Juana. She was telling the court that when Butch returned to Vallejo the night of the Derhammer murders, his favorite jeans were covered with blood.

"Butch," she told the court, "made me wash the jeans when he got home that night. They were his favorite pants. I scrubbed them by hand before I washed them in the machine."

His favorite jeans! In addition to his being cruel and

vicious, she was making him sound vain. She was laying it on. At least, Marko thought, he'd made the right choice about letting her come in on her own.

Then she told them about the Polaroid.

"I got my camera and took a picture of the jeans before I washed them."

"Where is that photograph now?" Blacklidge asked.

"It's here. It's in my purse," she said, opening her bag and pulling out the photo. "I wrote the date on the back."

She had taken a photograph of the bloody jeans, written the date on the back, had it with her! Oh, Angel, Marko thought. This was good—this was really good.

As Marko was chuckling to himself, Loftis jumped up from his chair.

"Your Honor, I object to introducing this photograph as evidence," the defense lawyer shouted. "There is no way we can say if these were Butch Crowley's jeans or even if this is real blood. We can't even say when the photo was taken," he added with a heavy dose of sarcasm. "Besides, we weren't given this photo in discovery; nor was this witness on the witness list."

"Gentlemen, please approach."

"Your Honor," Blacklidge said to the judge, "the State didn't know of the photograph until Miss Cruz testified about it. She was, in fact, a subpoenaed witness who had a late change of heart about coming in to testify."

Loftis huffed dismissively.

At which point, Judge Urso decided to let the jury decide about the veracity of the witness's testimony and the authenticity of the photo.

"This could be grounds for a mistrial, Your Honor," Loftis

said. Watching him, Marko thought the lawyer looked full of himself.

"If she is lying or the photograph isn't real, you can defend her at her perjury trial, counselor. My decision stands."

The judge held open the curtain, and Angel continued the show. For her encore, she brought out a grenade. She told the court what Butch had said as he shoved the bloody jeans at her: "It don't make you less of a man if you kill a little girl."

The exact words he'd spoken to Mapes.

Marko looked over at the defense table. Loftis's face flushed a bright red, further accentuated by his crisp white collar. And for the first time since the trial began, Butch's smirk began to fade.

———

DURING THE RECESS, Marko found Angel in the hallway outside the courtroom.

"You did great," Marko said. "You were fantastic."

"I told the truth."

"Set you free..."

"It feels like it. Anyway, I called Fabian yesterday. I wanted to thank him."

"For what?"

"Well, for helping me be the kind of person who could testify against Butch," Angel said.

Marko thought, only for the briefest second, What about me?

"So then Fabian says to me, 'Angel, I need an assistant. I want you to come back and work for me.'"

"Fabian—"

"And I said yes. The only reason I left Fabian and Juana was because I was afraid. Now, no matter where Butch ends up, I'm going back to Vegas."

Marko's favorite town.

64

FINALLY, IT WAS OVER. They'd finished. The trial lasted nine days—Monday through the following Thursday, with the weekend off. Now it was Friday, and the jury was out. Late yesterday afternoon they'd filed through the door next to the jury box, and they were sitting in a room, deliberating. Over the weekend, they would be sequestered.

Now Marko had to wait. It wasn't the kind of waiting he did when he was on surveillance. This time things were out of his hands, and that was a relief.

He tried to figure the odds on when they'd return a verdict. Nine days of testimony. A capital case. Four counts of murder in the first degree. Four counts of conspiracy to commit murder and arson. It wouldn't be soon. He needed to catch up, with both work and life, so he headed back to the Bay Area until the word came down that the verdict was in.

———

BACK IN NOVATO, he picked up the pile of mail from the floor by his front door, started throwing the circulars in the circular file, put the bills in a stack; then he found the thick, handwritten letter. It was obvious who the sender was. In the kitchen he found a knife, slit open the cream-colored envelope. He read it through quickly the first time, then read it again. He made some coffee, wandered around the house, went back to the kitchen, read the letter a third time, and started thinking back.

Over a year now since the murders in Fort Bragg, eight months since his trip to Vegas and the arrest near Bullhead City. A conclusion of sorts, yes, but when Marko got back home he knew that, really, the work had just begun. The prosecution of the case was still very much in front of them, and he could think of almost nothing else.

But that first weekend when he got back from Bullhead, it felt like returning home from war to the bosom of his lover. He and Marnie spent that whole first weekend together at his place, hardly getting out of bed. He felt good, celebratory. Marko knew that Marnie was the one, that he was in love with her. Saturday night they went to the restaurant in Larkspur Landing where they'd gone for their first date. They held hands. It felt like an anniversary. The whole weekend was special; it made him feel like he could look forward.

The next day he went to a little jewelry store on Grant Avenue in Old Town Novato, bought her a gold bracelet in a black-velvet box.

Looking back now, he remembered the sweetness, but also something else. Even that first weekend back home, in the midst of all the sex, the fun, and the intimacy, he had an almost subconscious sensation—call it a cop's intuition—even then he knew that something was different. Not that he could give it a name. Consciously, at the time, he thought that Marnie's hesitation was because she was still recovering from the attack.

In the months since, they still saw each other often, but Marnie had redoubled her work time, telling him she had to make up for what she'd lost. It was understandable. She was ambitious, she had fallen behind, she needed to regroup. Marko had been preoccupied with work too. The prosecution had to be very exacting. Blacklidge's team was demanding a lot from Marko, and that was in addition to all his other ATF work.

Now Marko knew what that cop's intuition was about. Now he had the proof in writing. The letter had arrived on one of the days he'd been in Ukiah. He was there every day of the trial, right behind the prosecution, most nights staying in a motel to avoid the commute from Novato, eating mediocre food at diners or wherever else time allowed. Even before he opened the letter, he knew what it was. Five handwritten pages on thick stationary. Marnie had written to him.

She spent the initial page and a half telling him how wonderful he was. Marnie, the diplomat, but meaning it, too. Next came the issues. First, his dangerous job, her fears that she wouldn't see him again, her inability to reach him when he was in the field. Then there had been Butch's attack, right outside her home—how she felt invaded, how her confidence had been eroded, how close she had come to losing her looks—the kiss of death for someone whose business was cosmetics.

Besides, she went on, Marko was a committed drinker and gambler, and she didn't want to end up penniless in old age with a beer-bellied man with red veins all over his face, with someone who didn't squander a moment thinking about the future. Just like her father.

She refused to spend the rest of her life worrying. It was

time to say good-bye, before either of them got in any deeper.

He read the letter dozens of times, trying to extract an understanding from it beyond its five pages. He knew that behind the words there was the reality of Edward. Safe, eligible Edward, with his money, his security, his ability to help Marnie with her career. Marnie, who'd grown up poor, had to fight for everything she'd achieved.

He understood her point of view. He didn't like it, but he understood. For Marnie, Marko's job made him an ineligible bachelor. His habits made him an unsuitable partner. But hadn't he put away his little black book? Stopped looking around at other women? Fallen in love with the girl of his dreams. Hadn't he decided there was only one woman for him?

And what about happiness? He thought they'd been happy. That was the point, wasn't it? Even a dumbshit like Marko had finally figured out that happiness was what it was all about.

Okay, he'd gotten the news, and it was bad. He decided that, for the moment, he needed to let it lay. After the Crowley verdict he would do whatever he could, but not now.

Now, at least, he thought he deserved some good news from the jurors.

65

THE JURY TOOK five days to decide Butch Crowley's fate. They deliberated on Friday, then on through the weekend, when they were sequestered in a hotel, then the following Monday and Tuesday. It was late Tuesday afternoon by the time the foreman notified the court that the verdict was unanimous.

The word went out to the attorneys, and Blacklidge called Gorky, who called Marko.

"They're back," Gorky said when Marko picked up.

"When?

"Blacklidge said Urso just announced it."

"So when do we hear?"

"Tomorrow at one, so the news guys and you city slickers can drive all the way up here and still be on time to hear it."

The next morning Marko put on his suit and tie and drove up to Ukiah. He'd arranged to meet Gorky beforehand for lunch at the diner across the street. They spent the first few minutes speculating about how it would be if the verdict went against them, but when lunch arrived, they stopped talking and concentrated on the food.

At twenty to one, the two of them headed across the street, taking the same seats they'd occupied for all nine days of the trial. The courtroom was packed, filled with the hum of expectation from spectators and the press. Marko was nervous about hearing the results of so much work and so much emotion. He knew Gorky was feeling the same way, because he could see him fidgeting.

Urso took his time getting into the courtroom, then they went through the usual pre-verdict protocol. Marko looked over at the twelve people in the jury box. To him, they were a cipher. They showed a lot of nervous energy, yes, but nothing in their faces or body language gave him even a hint about their decision. Those people who made a living out of predicting how potential jurors would decide—he wondered what they saw that he didn't.

Finally, the clerk handed the sheet of paper to Urso. The judge put on his reading glasses and cleared his throat. Marko took a deep breath, drummed his fingers on the edge of his seat. Urso looked over the courtroom, cleared his throat again.

It was like the final seconds of a close game. One minute you're wringing your hands, the next you're either jumping for joy or hanging your head.

This time, victory was in Marko's corner.

Suddenly, he was flooded with relief. He wanted to shout a resounding Yes! He wanted to walk to the defense table and pump his fist in Butch's face.

He didn't, of course. And he didn't shout, though there were several in the room who did.

The jury, Judge Urso told the court, had found Butch Crowley guilty on all counts.

———————

IT WASN'T UNTIL the following Wednesday that Judge Urso was ready to pass sentence on Butch Crowley. Because it was a capital case, the defense laid out all the reasons why Butch's life should be spared. The physical and mental abuse he suffered as a child, his parents' alcoholism, his abandonment by his mother and, later, by his abusive father. How, because of these traumas, he developed a narcissistic personality, had trouble problem-solving, was impulsive, lacked self-discipline, was unable to change a course of action once he had set it, was unable to read his immediate environment and respond appropriately. It went on and on. They called it mitigation.

Marko heard it all, not without sympathy. He'd been raised a Catholic, with everything that went along with it, all still very much with him. He thought of his devout parents, who had wanted him to become a priest; he thought of his four siblings and their families, all of them going to mass every Sunday. But as he sat there waiting to hear the sentence, he could feel himself hoping that Urso would put an end to Butch's life on earth.

And not just that. First he wanted Butch to suffer, then he wanted Butch to get a needle in the arm that would finally stop his cold-blooded heart. And Marko wanted to be there when it happened. He wanted to shove the photo of little Dallas up against the glass of the execution chamber so that it would be the last thing Butch ever saw.

That's how Marko had been imagining it for the past week, since the verdict had been read, and that's what he felt in his heart was fair.

Well, it wasn't going to happen.

Judge Urso gave Gerald "Butch" Crowley life in prison without the possibility of parole.

Butch Crowley had been defeated. Not like Marko had hoped, but still, Butch had gone down. And maybe living in prison, in hell, for the rest of his days was the greater punishment.

The next day Marko left for Vegas.

LAS VEGAS

66

WHEN MARKO GOT off the plane at McCarran, he wanted to kiss the ground. He spent his first couple of hours in Vegas walking around the Strip in shirt sleeves, feeling the warm afternoon air, taking in the sights like a first-time tourist. By the time he got back to the hotel, the light was fading, and he was ready for the evening to begin.

In his third-floor room, Marko unpacked his jacket and reached in the pocket where he'd put the picture of Dallas Derhammer. He took out the photo and looked at it, deciding it would be for the last time. The ordeal was over. It was time to move on. Marko wanted to clear every thought of the Derhammer murders from his head, file the case in the back of his brain, and not look at it again for a very long time. He was sick of thinking about justice and everything that went along with it.

He was also sick of thinking about Marnie.

No, that wasn't true. He *wished* he was sick of thinking about Marnie. Actually, he wanted to think about her more than he had time for. And right now he had a lot of time. It had been almost two weeks since he'd gotten her Dear John letter. There were a lot of good reasons for what she wrote. Marko knew them better than she did, but he wished at least they'd been able to have a conversation about them.

———————

THAT NIGHT, Marko bought a twenty-dollar pay-per-view ticket to watch the Chavez-Rosario fight on the big screen at the Las Vegas Hilton. Tickets for the actual fight were sold out, and, anyway, they were way too expensive.

Julio Cesar Chavez and his nine siblings grew up in an abandoned railroad car. He began boxing early, found he had the speed, the reflexes, and the will to win, and became a professional for the money. "I saw my mom working, ironing and washing peoples' clothes," he said one time in an interview that Marko had read. "I promised her I would give her a house someday and she would never have that job again."

For the big fight in Vegas, Chavez moved up in weight class to face Edwin Rosario, the WBA Lightweight Champion. The money was mostly on Chavez, with his nine title defenses, even though there was concern about how he'd handle the move up in weight against hard-punching Rosario.

When Marko got to the pay-per-view, the room was buzzing. He could feel the excitement. As soon as the fight started, the crowd went wild with every punch. Chavez took the upper hand early, then it became completely his night. Rosario couldn't weather the body shots he was getting from Chavez, and his right eye was completely swollen shut so that he couldn't see Chavez's right hand. When Rosario's corner finally threw in the towel, a cool and calm Chavez raised his arms in triumph. He beat Edwin Rosario in eleven rounds on a TKO, a career-defining victory.

The crowd and the victory left Marko feeling high. After the fight, he milled around with the other fans, refought each round, analyzed the win. Later, he took a stroll through the casino, smiling to himself, humming a Teddy Pendergrass tune called "Love T.K.O." Was that what had happened to him, a love T.K.O.? Was it the end with Marnie, was she gone forever, should he let it go? Or would she come back, like Angel? At the moment, he didn't have a clue.

At the far end of the huge, high-ceilinged, smoky, noisy room were the blackjack tables. He found a table he liked, one with a ten-dollar minimum, the dealer smiling at him as he pulled up a stool at third base.

Nothing better.

It was all here—a comfortable place to sit, the chips neatly stacked, a holder for his drink, the jingle-jangle of the slots for background music. His own little green-felt paradise, nothing to think about but the cards.

Marko put down his action money, got his chips, and for the first time in a while felt lucky. Right off, he caught a short streak and went into the black. When he was up two hundred dollars, he decided to go for it and press his bets.

He was playing two greens a hand and doubling down every chance. The dealer dealt him two eights, which he split against her show six. Then two more paint cards for Marko. The dealer busted, and he toked her a greenie.

He lost four hands in a row, but then the dealer cooled off, and Marko caught another streak. He knew the probabilities, that sooner or later the cards would turn bad, but also that a good situation could last a while—and he let himself feel happy being on the upside.

A cute little red-lipped cocktail waitress walked by carrying a tray. She was wearing a low-cut black outfit with a short skirt. The outfit was just like what all the other cocktail waitresses wore, but on her it looked special. For that moment, she was the only girl in the world.

Just for that moment, he had everything he needed.

Marko raised his glass to her. She smiled at him, came over.

It was time to order a double.

ACKNOWLEDGMENTS

Mark Rusin

I am one of the luckiest people I know. I have truly lived the American Dream, having been brought up by two wonderful, loving parents, Richard and Adeline. My parents brought up their five kids in a small bungalow near Midway Airport in Chicago. I have three sisters, Marsha, Cindy, and Sheila, and one brother, Cliff.

Growing up in the late fifties and sixties in a vibrant city like Chicago brought out the civic pride and ethnicity for all. Back then, there was no such thing as a hate crime. You just got caught in the wrong neighborhood and that was that. The ass-kicking you got was considered deserved and a reinforcement to stay the hell away from that neighborhood.

I vividly recall exactly where I was in 1958 when all the adults were crying and I didn't know why. Turns out ninety-five people, including ninety-two kids, were killed in the fire at Our Lady of Angels Catholic School. When I was just four I recall one September night in 1959 when air-raid sirens could be heard throughout the city, and they seemed especially loud in our basement where all us kids went to hide. My dad picked me up and said, "The White Sox just won the pennant, it's okay." I had no clue what a pennant was, but my dad's huge arms wrapped around me and his saying "it's okay" was good enough for me.

Then the Bears won it all in 1963, but President Kennedy was killed, so the Bears' accomplishment really took a back seat. The Bulls came to be in 1966, and crazy Richard Speck killed all those nurses that same year. I will never forget rolling the Sun-Times and Tribunes the morning after he got caught. I was a paperboy at age eleven.

In 1967 McCormack Place burned down, and then in April 1968 Dr. King was shot and killed. A couple of months later Bobby Kennedy was killed in Los Angeles. There were the race riots during the election in 1968, and the Cubs folded to the Amazing Mets in the fall of 1969. Those were the days.

Then off to high school and college where ice hockey became my passion. I could really shoot the puck but my skating wasn't good enough. I was also intrigued with law enforcement at that time. I figured I could help people and not be stuck to a desk. In the end, I was right and it was the best move of my life, next to asking my wife, Marcie, to marry me.

Here I would like to acknowledge and say thanks to all the cops and firefighters in America. These are the real heroes. When the bell rings they go. They routinely put their own lives on the line for strangers. I still get a kick out of all those Monday-morning quarterbacks who are first to criticize a cop or fireman. I say go put on a uniform and let's see how you do.

I also would like to acknowledge Priscilla Barton for helping me to get this book published. She turned this short police story into a crime novel. Priscilla is a talented and hard-working professional to whom I will always be grateful.

To my wife, Marcie, who supported me to write my story

and who played an invaluable role in the publishing of this book.

Lastly, to my friends and colleagues over the years. You all know who you are. Thank you all.

Priscilla Barton

I am grateful to my Santa Fe writers' group—Cia Khakaura, Shelleen McQueen, George Papcun, and Victor Atyas—for their insightful comments on the manuscript and their sense of fun. My warmest thanks to Judith Toler and Liz Tuck--good friends, perceptive critics, astute editors.

Thanks also to Dr. Philip Bradford, M.D., for providing medical details relevant to gunshot wounds, to the Mohave County Sheriff's Department for information on police procedure in that county, and to Albert Ortiz, Jr., and Brian McGinnis of the Oracle Fire Department for their instructive comments on search-and-rescue and EMT practices.

My abiding gratitude to Hector Lovemore, favorite reader, for his patience, love, support, and enviable good humor, his invaluable information on mining and mine safety, and his insights into the writing process at every level.

ABOUT THE AUTHORS

Mark Rusin was born and raised on the south side of Chicago. He attended Quigley South High School and Western Illinois University, where he majored in law-enforcement administration (and ice hockey.) Mark is a former Las Vegas Metropolitan Police Officer and retired ATF Special Agent. During his law-enforcement career, Mark witnessed and investigated several major fire scenes, homicides, bombings, and other high-profile cases, which serve as inspiration for his stories. He is a Chicago sports junkie and a published writer. This is his first crime novel. Mark lives in the Chicago area with his wife, Marcie, where he continues to write stories and still dreams about playing hockey for his hometown Blackhawks.

Priscilla Barton is a writer based in the Southwest, who has also worked as a film curator, book editor, and agitprop artist. A member of Sisters in Crime, she divides her time between the high-desert country of southern Arizona and Santa Fe, New Mexico.

44853360R00148

Made in the USA
San Bernardino, CA
25 January 2017